CORVO HOLLOWS

A Psychological Thriller

April A. Taylor

Cover designed by James, GoOnWrite.com

This book is a work of fiction. Names, characters, places, and incidents either are products of the author's imagination or are used fictitiously. Any resemblance to actual persons, living or dead, events, or locales is entirely coincidental.

April A. Taylor
Visit my website at www.AprilATaylor.net

Printed in the United States of America

First Printing: March 2019
Midnight Grasshopper Books

ISBN:

978-1-09-033176-2

PRAISE FOR THE AUTHOR'S PREVIOIUS WORKS

"A spectacular read...absolutely gripping. I couldn't force myself to put it down. Taylor did an excellent and meticulous job creating this story, forming imagery...invoking real emotion on the part of the reader."
- *The Horror Report*

"Takes [the] standard genre template and turns it upside-down...the crazy whirlwind that ensues is enough to make even the biggest horror fan a bit dizzy...unique...with a literary approach that combines modern and mid-twentieth century techniques." - *Inquisitr, The Best Horror Books of 2018*

"Grief is the driving force in *The Haunting of Cabin Green*. Taylor weaves a haunting tale of a man who can't be sure if the desolate cabin he's staying in is full of ghosts or if his mind is playing tricks on him."
- *Popsugar, The 13 Most Chilling Horror Books of 2018*

"Unique... the author depicts the grieving process amazingly well. The story is claustrophobic... and what an ending. All of the flashbacks and delusions suddenly make sense... [it's a] sucker punch."
- *HorrorTalk.com*

BIBLIOGRAPHY

Psychological Thriller

Corvo Hollows

Alexa Bentley Paranormal Mysteries

Book One – Missing in Michigan
Book Two – Frightened in France
Book Three – Lost in Louisiana

Midnight Myths and Fairy Tales Series

Book One – Vasilisa the Terrible: A Baba Yaga Story
Book Two – Death Song of the Sea: A Celtic Story

Horror

The Haunting of Cabin Green: A Modern Gothic Horror Novel

This book is for the real-life "Anna" and for everyone else battling an invisible illness such as fibromyalgia.

CHAPTER ONE

An unseen woman's ragged screams had just split the air inside Anna's apartment. She hesitated imperceptibly before jumping to her feet. Without a single thought for her own safety, the tall brunette threw the front door open and peered outside.

The harsh July sun beat down on the pavement and reflected off the neighbor's wind chimes. Sun spots obscured Anna's vision, and she lifted her hand to her eyes in a bid to wipe away the visual disturbances.

Her sight started to clear just as the disorienting and terrifying screams returned. A middle-aged woman with ratty hair, disheveled clothing, and bare feet reached toward her from about one-hundred feet away. Anna's gaze fell first to the woman's bloody feet. Then she spotted a black pickup truck and its elderly male driver. His long, gray hair threatened to fly free of his head as he sprung out of the newly parked vehicle.

The woman rapidly advanced upon Anna's doorstep before stopping unexpectedly. Her body shook with the force of her recent exertions, and she appeared poised to scream yet again.

"What's wrong? Do you need help? I can call the police," Anna said in a jumbled mess.

The woman's eyes darted from Anna to the front door. She took a deep breath and said, "Yes, I need help! Please, let me in!"

All of Anna's instincts screamed as she patted her pockets in search of her phone. *Dammit*, she thought. Her phone was nestled safely inside the apartment.

A quick scan of the environment showed Anna that the mysterious man hadn't come any closer. In fact, he stood calmly by the side of the truck and appeared to be watching them with interest. Anna made eye contact with him, and it sent a shiver down her spine.

Something isn't right.

"Look, I'm going to call the police for you, okay?"

"But I already called them. They're on their way," the woman pouted.

"I'm going to call again, just to make sure. Stay there." Anna motioned for the woman to remain at her current position, approximately twenty feet away.

A strange smile flitted across the woman's lips, and it accentuated the wrinkles around her mouth. She took one step forward, then another.

"Please stay there," Anna said as sweat trickled down her back and her mind exploded with anxiety.

"This is public property, ma'am," the woman responded while taking two more steps. "I have a right to be here."

Anna's sense of unease officially ballooned into an overwhelming tide of panic. Unsure what to do, she risked turning her back on the woman long enough to re-enter her apartment. That was the plan, anyway. With one firm pull, followed by three successive tugs, she was met by the sickening realization that her screen door had somehow jammed shut.

Stay calm, stay calm. Don't show fear.

Anna glanced over her shoulder and found the woman a mere five feet away, her face transformed by the lupine features of an alpha animal on the prowl. The man stood a few feet closer, too, and his hard stare belied his attempt at casual indifference.

It's now or never.

One last, victorious tug broke the door free of its humidity-induced prison. She tumbled gracelessly through the entrance and slammed the door in the woman's face.

Each lock clicked into place as Anna placed her back to the door and slid to her knees. Her breathing raged out of control; hyperventilation had become a foregone conclusion, so she steered into the skid and allowed it to happen.

A few minutes later, she composed herself enough to grab her phone. As her fingers danced across the keypad, she slowly pulled apart two slats in the mini blinds. No one was there, nor was there any sign of the black truck.

"911. What's your emergency?"

* * * * *

Detective Stan Brodsky stood uncomfortably in his suit. Although it was eight o'clock in the evening, the heat index still hovered around one-hundred degrees Fahrenheit. He'd already had a long, arduous day of dealing with an unusual-and still unsolved-murder, not to mention the steady stream of overwrought residents who apparently believed 911 was their personal hotline for airing grievances.

The woman sitting in front of him hadn't deviated from her story during three retellings. He could also sense her fear; it had been more than an hour since the alleged incident, but the tension in the air was still palpable. Although he and his partner, Detective Samuel Jones, hadn't found any corroborating evidence, they also had no reason not to believe her story, especially in light of recent local events.

"Okay, ma'am, we're going to file a report, and we'll have a cruiser ride through here a few times a day for the next week or so. It sounds like they were attempting a burglary, so be sure to lock your house and car doors. And let us know if you see them again," Brodsky said while handing Anna an off-white business card.

She looked at it thoughtfully, as if it alone could somehow protect her. "Are you sure it's safe to be here, officer? Should I go to a hotel or something instead?"

"Detective. And you should definitely do what makes you feel comfortable, ma'am. But in my experience, perps like this don't often return to the scene of their failed attempt. You're on guard now, and they know it. They also know you probably called the police. No, it's much easier for them to go elsewhere."

Unfortunately, he thought. He didn't want anything to happen to her, of course. He just wished for once criminals would make his life less complicated. After all, if they kept trying to commit crimes in the same places, his job would be a breeze. He could issue as many platitudes as needed to make people like Anna feel better, especially because the burglars she'd encountered would almost certainly skip town and slip through the cracks. Again.

"Okay," she responded.

He could practically see the cogs spinning in her brain. It was clear she wouldn't be getting much sleep tonight. He decided to take one last stab at calming her down.

"You did the right thing, ma'am. You've got good instincts. I tell you what, if you think you hear or see something out of the ordinary, call us. Anytime, day or night. Dispatch will patch you through to the closest officer if I'm not on duty."

"Oh, but I don't want to trouble you for nothing..."

"It's no trouble, ma'am. Seriously. This is what we're here for."

"Thanks," she said shyly as the officers started making their way toward the door.

"He's right, ma'am," Jones said while exiting the house. "Always listen to your instincts. Have a good night."

The two detectives waited until they were back in their unmarked car to share their true feelings.

"Do you really think it was a burglar?" Jones asked.

"Probably," Brodsky replied.

"Then why did dispatch patch the call through to homicide?"

"Aside from the department being ridiculously understaffed right now?" Brodsky pushed his hair back from his forehead. "I'd say they thought this might be connected to the killer from earlier. And maybe they're right."

CHAPTER TWO

"It was terrible," Anna concluded. She'd just shared the tale of her creepy encounter again.

Her therapist, Jeani, nodded her head sympathetically. "That *does* sound horrible. And terrifying. I'm so glad you're okay. Tell me more about the steps you're taking to regain your sense of safety within your home."

Of course, Anna thought. She liked her therapist, but she sometimes wished they would talk about her issues without using such a blatant, textbook approach to psychology.

"I contacted the community manager, and he agreed to install an extra lock on my front door. The maintenance guy also replaced the screen door so that it doesn't stick anymore. Aside from that, I've made sure to keep all the doors and windows locked up tight. Not that I'd open them much right now anyway, mind you," she deflected. "It's way too hot out. Speaking of heat, did you see the latest news reports about climate change?"

Jeani smiled indulgently. Anna loved to go off topic whenever possible, which was a classic avoidance technique. Jenni occasionally let her client do this for a few moments before pulling her back to the issue at hand.

"I did see a news story about that. Scary stuff, huh? But that's a much bigger, and far less controllable, topic. Let's narrow in on your more immediately pressing concerns. Tell me, have you been getting much sleep?"

Anna considered lying, but she knew Jeani would see right through it. Thanks to her raccoon eyes, anyone could see the truth plainly written on her face, unless they were the most unobservant creature on the planet.

"Not really. But I was having the same issue before any of this happened, remember?"

"Yes, I do. Are you having any flashbacks or thoughts about the incident before falling asleep?"

Like a dog with a bone, Anna sighed.

"As a matter of fact, yes, I am. But it's nothing I can't deal with, you know?"

"I absolutely believe you can deal with it, Anna," her therapist said gently. "But this is something you don't have to keep carrying around. I'm here to help you, if you'll let me."

Anna glanced at the clock hanging slightly askew on the far wall. Next, her eyes fell on the woman in front of her. Jeani had a big heart, a psychologically-driven mind, and a shockingly bright red head of hair. She was the type of woman you couldn't help but notice, and empathy had a permanent parking space in her eyes.

At the same time, she often adhered too closely to her beloved tools of the trade.

Jeani had provided an open ear and a mostly unjudgmental environment for a couple of years, but she still hadn't completely broken through all of Anna's defense mechanisms. These had been hard earned, and Anna took an almost perverse sense of pleasure in knowing that Jeani's latest efforts weren't going to have the full intended effect because the hour was almost up.

Anna eyed the clock. "Same time next week?"

"Yes. In the meantime, don't forget to use your breathing exercises, along with journaling. And remember that exercising always lifts your mood! Perhaps you'd even like to take a self-defense course?"

Anna thanked Jeani and headed toward the door.

"I'm always here if you need me, Anna. Call me if you want to get in sooner."

Anna nodded her head, but she knew there was no way she'd be back before next week. And even that was debatable, as the self-destructive part of her had already begun coming up with excuses for canceling her next session.

CHAPTER THREE

Anna's eyes leaked with tiredness, so she tossed her iPad on the side table and stretched out across her queen-sized bed. A gentle breeze from the ceiling fan she had nicknamed Cthulhu – because it terrified her cats – kept wicking away the sweat from her face. Despite the heat, she pulled a thin sheet across most of her body and felt the sweet relief of finally relaxing enough to fall asleep.

* * * * *

Anna flew out of bed like it was on fire. Sweat drenched her body as she gasped for air. Her heart threatened to punch a hole in her chest. Reaching to the bedside table, she grabbed her black, wire-thin glasses and haphazardly put them on.

What was that?

The pervasive darkness that only black-out curtains could provide prevented her from seeing anything. She closed her eyes, cocked her head to the side, and attempted to reach out into the darkness with all of her other senses. The air had a heavy feeling, which she knew was a mixture of fear and humidity, but there were no sounds or other sensations to justify the rapid pace of her pulse.

Anna wasn't ready to commit to fully lying down again, but she pressed her back against the headboard and took a deep breath. After a few more breaths, her body's fight or flight system disengaged – as much as it ever did, that is. Unlike most people, she had the perfect storm of past experiences and medical issues, and it made her unable to ever truly relax because her mind always remained alert.

Satisfied that the noise she thought she's heard had originated inside her dreamland, Anna's eyes closed once again.

BAM! BAM! BAM!

Her headboard shook with an impact that reverberated throughout the bedroom. One of her cats leapt off the bed and dashed into the hallway. All the deep breathing exercises in the world wouldn't have been enough to calm her rapidly re-escalating heartbeat as she jumped free of her sheet once more.

She pulled on her thin blue robe, grabbed a tiny flashlight, and headed into the hallway. Annoyance and fear rippled across her face as the banging noise returned for yet another round. Concentrating closely, she traced the source of the noise to her back inner wall, which didn't make any sense at all.

The lone apartment adjacent to that wall had been empty for more than a month. How in the world was someone over there in the middle of the night? And, more importantly, what were they doing?

The right side of her head pressed against the cream-colored wall as she listened for more evidence that something was amiss. When nothing else happened for more than ten minutes, she found herself doubting that she'd actually heard anything at all. Unsure how – or if – to proceed, she headed back to bed.

This time, sleep remained elusive, so she turned on her bedside lamp and picked up her iPad again. Anna's talent for art had been apparent from a young age. By the time she turned seven, she had become inseparable from her art supplies. Her parents had scoffed at the idea that art could be a viable career, but she'd proven them wrong.

Her work crossed multiple mediums, including pencils, paints, charcoal, and digital art. Regular pencils would always be her first love, but digital art had changed her life.

The electronic pencil in her left hand had allowed her to build a solid reputation as a cover designer, and her work currently adorned books aimed at readers between the ages of eight and twelve. She'd slowed down some over the past year – the inevitable and depressing result of hand pain caused by fibromyalgia – but that didn't prevent her from continuing to make a living with her creativity.

She couldn't stop chewing over the mysterious noises. After several minutes, her eyes and mind finally clicked back together and she took in her latest piece. A spooky image of a man hiding in shadows stared back at her. A cold chill defied the hot, muggy night by running down her back. She had no idea who the man was or where the idea to draw him had come from.

CHAPTER FOUR

"Look, I'm telling you what I heard, okay? It happened twice and scared my cats half to death," Anna said into the iPhone pressed against her ear.

"I'll send maintenance over to check it out. Something probably just fell. Or maybe a critter got into the walls," the bored-sounding apartment manager replied from the other side of the line.

"Thank you," she said before realizing the line had already gone dead.

That figures.

Anna hated to complain – in fact, she hated everything about talking on the phone – but she'd woken up concerned about squatters. Although she lived in one of the nicest cities in the Metro Detroit area, she knew that homelessness was still prevalent.

A yawn slipped out of her mouth as her arms stretched into the air. Yet another night with broken, fitful sleep had left her exhausted, like usual. The only available remedy was caffeine, and lots of it. Anna turned on the coffeemaker, and the aroma of freshly brewed wakefulness soon permeated the small kitchen. Her eyes finally opened more than halfway for the first time that day.

Anna's body stiffened as footsteps echoed from the apartment behind hers, but she quickly chided herself after remembering that the maintenance man should be there by now. John wasn't much of a talker, but he did a decent job of keeping everything in good shape. She trusted him to ferret out the cause of last night's disturbances.

With nothing else of importance to do, she wandered into her art studio. Drawings and paintings from throughout her life spanned almost every inch of wall space. She had to walk carefully between the rows of easels to reach her work desk.

Anna sat in her comfortable office chair and looked at her current work in progress. She'd been hired to draw a digital cover image in the same basic style as artistic genius Stephen Gammell's work from the *Scary Stories to Tell in the Dark* series.

Gammell's illustrations had terrified her as a child, but they'd also left an indelible imprint on her that altered her career for the better. Even when she worked with much more cheerful imagery – which was usually the case – she still drew inspiration from Gammell's masterful usage of shading.

That's probably where last night's sketch came from, she mused as her creative spark lit brightly once again. She tuned out everything else around her – like always – while working diligently on each tiny detail. She probably wouldn't have even remembered to stop a couple of hours later for lunch if her cats hadn't started complaining loudly about wanting more food.

With new kibble in their bowls, the cats went to town gorging themselves as Anna nibbled on apple slices covered with peanut butter. She took her phone off the charger and checked the screen. She'd missed a phone call and a voicemail, but this wasn't surprising since she'd once been told that a nuclear explosion wouldn't even distract her from her work.

Frowning, she read through the iPhone's speech-to-text translation of the message. According to John, nothing seemed unusual in the apartment behind hers. The front door had still been locked and there were no signs of squatters or critters.

Anna went into her bedroom, put on some fresh clothes, and walked outside to investigate matters for herself. It only took a minute to navigate around the building. She knew everyone else in the area would be gone to work, but she still took a few seconds to look around before walking up to the apartment's living room window. She cupped her hands around her eyes to block out the blazing sun and pressed her face to the window, expecting to see something that John had missed.

There was nothing there. The unit stood completely empty, and she could see dust particles floating through the dining room light that John must have inadvertently left on. A thin coating of dust had also settled on all the visible areas.

What the hell?

Shaken, but still not entirely convinced of the apartment's innocence, she walked back to her side of the six-unit building while trying not to melt under the sun's fierce gaze.

Maybe I need to get out of here for a little while.

Such thoughts were unusual for Anna, who vastly preferred the comfort of her own space over being out in public. Her doctor and therapist called it everything from "social anxiety" to "PTSD," and they also blamed it on the depression and fatigue associated with chronic pain. She referred to it by a more simplistic phrase: being a hermit.

She knew she had to take advantage of the rare moments when she actually wanted to voyage past her front door, so she decided to head toward the closest bookstore. Unfortunately, that meant driving almost seven miles away, when it used to be something she could find by merely going around the corner.

She slipped inside her old Saturn and heard the engine complain slightly as she turned the key. There wasn't actually anything wrong with it, but the battery often needed a little prompting since she didn't drive very often.

A familiar rush of anxiety flooded her body. She sat in the parking lot battling the urge to bolt free of the car and go back to her studio. In the end, she convinced herself to move forward with her planned trip because she hadn't seen her latest book cover in a physical store yet.

She approached the end of the community – just past the 'Welcome to Corvo Hollows' sign – and her eyes automatically flitted to the rearview mirror. A small black pickup truck filled the frame. It signaled that it also wanted to turn right onto the main road.

A couple of opportunities presented themselves, but she waited until she felt fully confident to turn into traffic. The driver behind her hadn't honked their horn, but they had revved their engine after she missed the second chance to pull out.

The drive to the large strip mall with an attached Barnes & Noble passed uneventfully. The parking lot sat almost empty, which simultaneously made her cheer and frown. She always embraced any chance to shop without being in a big crowd, but she also hated how difficult it had become for brick and mortar bookstores to make a profit.

Anna waited at the crosswalk that connected the parking lot with the front of the building. A small black pickup truck moved quickly down the strip mall drive and she blinked twice in recognition. Fear crept into the back of her throat again and threatened to strangle her.

Don't be ridiculous. There's got to be thousands of trucks like that around here.

Unsure if the vehicle had followed her or was nothing more than a coincidence, she tentatively entered the crosswalk and continued toward her intended destination. A rush of very welcome cool air swirled around her as she entered the store. This, combined with the excitement of seeing her artwork on the cover of yet another children's book, whisked away all lingering thoughts of the truck.

CHAPTER FIVE

Sleep came easily to Anna for the first time in months. No noises disturbed her, and she woke long after the sun rose to cast its brutal rays on Metro Detroit once again. Disoriented, she looked at her phone through blurry eyes and saw a couple texts from her sister, Liz. Firing off a quick response, she headed to the bathroom to begin her morning routine.

One hour later, a harsh rapping made her stomach jump.

Dammit, Liz. Why do you always have to do that?

Liz's knock was like a cross between a police officer's and a frantic neighbor begging for help, and it chilled Anna's insides each time she heard it. Taking a deep breath and setting a smile on her face, Anna opened the door to greet her sister.

"Hi, sis! Come on in," she said.

"I brought pizza!" Liz announced as she burst into the room.

"Oh, great! Did you remember to get it with white sauce?"

"Are you still on that? No, of course not. Who the hell eats pizza without loading it with a spicy tomato sauce?" Liz asked, making Anna feel about two inches tall.

"Come on, Liz. We've talked about this. You know pizza sauce makes my fibro stuff worse."

"Not this again," Liz groaned. "You know, my friend Melissa said that fibro...meahlgera," she butchered the word, as usual, "isn't real. It's all in your head, sister." Liz tapped the side of her head to emphasize her point.

I love my sister, I love my sister, I love my sister, Anna thought, in an attempt to calm down. It didn't work.

"I'd rather take medical advice from actual doctors instead of Doctor Google," she said quietly but firmly.

"What?" Liz said with a hurt expression. "Melissa really knows her stuff. Maybe you should talk to her about it. She might be able to help."

Right. That's why she buys into every new conspiracy theory.

"No thanks," Anna scoffed.

"Can't we ever have a nice, normal visit?" Liz asked.

Anna took in Liz's pleading eyes and all the fight fled her body. As the older sister, she still felt a sense of duty toward Liz, no matter how wayward she believed her thoughts and friends were.

"You're right," Anna said as she grabbed some plates and napkins, along with a fork for herself. "Thanks for bringing lunch."

They both pulled a slice of piping hot cheese pizza from its cardboard home. Liz saturated hers with salt and pepper. Meanwhile, Anna used her fork to peel the cheese up and started scraping off as much of the sauce as possible.

As they ate, Liz babbled on and on about every little thing that popped into her head. The conversation vacillated from last night's showing of her favorite TV show all the way to something gruesome she'd heard on the news.

"They said the heads were completely ripped off," Liz finished as Anna's focus shifted back into place.

"Wait, what? Tell me that last story again."

Exasperated, Liz said, "I swear, Anna. Your head is permanently in the clouds. I bet you didn't hear anything else I said."

With a pout, Liz picked out the largest slice of pizza and inhaled it.

"No, I did. I promise. I just kind of spaced out there for a second at the end."

Liz appraised her sister's countenance in an attempt to find any signs of duplicity or remorse. Apparently satisfied, she repeated her story.

"Like I said, the news on Channel 7 was abuzz this morning with yet another murder. And not in Detroit, like usual. No, this happened on the other side of town, of all places. They found a body, but the head was missing! That's the second one this week, too. Can you imagine?"

Anna couldn't unimagine it. Her sister's words sparked her fear once again, and before she knew it, words were tumbling out of her mouth.

"That reminds me...did I tell you about what happened here the other day?"

Anna knew she hadn't, but she needed a way to broach the subject.

"No," Liz said with her eyes wide. "What? What happened?"

Liz was practically salivating at the idea of getting some good gossip. Anna proceeded to recount all the details. After she finished, her sister adopted a skeptical visage.

"It sounds like they just needed help or something."

"What? How could you possibly come to that conclusion?"

"Well, I mean...you did say they were a white couple, right?"

Oh, my fucking god. Not this shit again.

"Yes. Yes, I did. And even the cops think they were trying to break in or something, so don't get started, okay?"

Liz looked at her like she'd been slapped.

"What do you mean?" she retorted indignantly.

Deciding to take a different angle, Anna said, "Even the police believe they were up to no good. The officers told me they were probably trying to break into my house. But honestly? It felt much more...*sinister* than that."

Liz sat far back in her chair and peered at Anna as if she were trying to mentally fit her with a straightjacket.

"Sinister?" she laughed. "Sounds like you've been spending too much time reading those nonsense thriller novels and working on your latest job. I don't know why in the world you'd take on a scary project like that, but it's clearly messing with you."

Against her better judgment, Anna rushed to defend herself.

"First off, this has *nothing* to do with my work. And secondly, there were a bunch of crazy noises coming from next door that night, too. But no one lives there. How do you explain *that*?"

"I think you're overworked, sis. Maybe you need to see a headshrinker or something."

Anna had never told any of her family members about her visits to a therapist. The usage of the denigrating term 'headshrinker' was exactly what she'd expected from them, especially Liz.

Sure, she believes in a nutjob's theories, but not in counseling. How typical.

"I'm *fine*," Anna said with thinly veiled impatience. "Look, thanks for bringing over lunch, but I really need to get back to work."

Liz's eyes filled with hurt, and she reached for her sister's hand.

"Aw, come on. Don't be like that, Anna. You know I'm just messing around."

No, you're not.

"It's okay," Anna lied. "We're fine. I do really need to get to work, though."

Somewhat reassured by Anna's false words, Liz got up, gave her sister a hug, and said, "We should get together again soon. Oh, and keep the leftovers!"

As soon as the door had been closed and locked, Anna's face fell from fake happiness into anger.

"Bitch," she muttered under her breath.

She stalked over to the pizza that was already upsetting her stomach and making her joints ache. With only a second of contemplation, she tossed the entire box in the trash.

CHAPTER SIX

Anna had just reached the terrifying reveal in a crime thriller she'd started a couple weeks ago when the real world harshly intruded. She sat indecisively for a moment, unable to figure out if the scream she'd just heard was real life or merely an echo from inside the fictional universe she'd been lost in for the past twenty minutes. When another scream threatened to split her eardrums, she jumped out of her recliner in a hurry.

She placed her hand on the wall that abutted the empty unit behind hers. It moved ever so slightly beneath her touch as something unseen wacked against it. With a sickening crunch, the screams came to an instant halt.

Oh my god, oh my god, oh my god. What do I do?

Calling 911 might have been the most sensical move, but instead, she leapt to her fridge and pulled Brodsky's card from behind a Detroit Zoo magnet. Her fingers fumbled for the right numbers, and she had to hit end and redial twice before getting the correct combination.

The cold, mechanical tone on the other end made her miss the old days when business ringtones didn't sound machine-like.

Come on, come on! Pick up!

On the fourth ring, she heard a weary but professional voice announce, "Detective Brodsky, how can I help?"

Swallowing a hard, dry lump of fear that had formed in the back of her throat, Anna managed to squeak out her concerns.

"Officer Brodsky? This is Anna Collins. From the other day? I think something terrible just happened."

"Anna? Yes, this is Detective Brodsky. What's going on?"

"I heard a loud scream again, you know, like before? But this time it was coming from the apartment behind mine. She screamed and screamed, but then something hit the wall really hard...and, well, I didn't hear anything else after that."

Tears filled her eyes as the adrenaline coursing through her veins gave way to the realization that she might have just heard a domestic assault. Or worse.

"I'm on my way. And ma'am? Lock your doors and stay inside."

"Yes, Detective," she said to a dial tone.

* * * * *

Brodsky hopped into his unmarked police vehicle without stopping to tell anyone else what he'd just heard. He did, however, send a quick text to his partner to help ensure backup would be on the way soon. He understood the odds were against Anna having heard anything more than yet another domestic violence case, but after what had been found this morning, he couldn't take any chances.

He made it down Ford Road and entered the Corvo Hollows community again for the second time in less than a week. With Anna's words ringing in his ears, he jumped out of the car and unbuttoned his gun holster.

Brodsky's black shoes squished in the mud caused by an errant sprinkler as he attempted to move unnoticed down the sidewalk. In the wintertime, this would have been a breeze in the poorly lit neighborhood. But right now, the sun still illuminated everything, even though it was seven-thirty in the evening.

The last of the row of three garden-style apartments drew closer. He moved his tall, solid frame against the side of the building and ducked down to get past the large bedroom windows. His steady breathing showcased his experience with situations like this, but he'd be lying if he tried to claim his pulse hadn't sped up a bit by the time he approached the front door.

He banged on the door with his most authoritative knock, followed by barking, "Open up! This is the police!"

Brodsky listened closely but heard nothing emanating from this particular unit. He carefully crept over to the living room window and saw the entire room was empty. After checking the remaining two windows, he exhaled, relocked his holster, and sauntered over to the next apartment where a woman in her early forties peered at him from behind a screen door. She had the appearance and general air of a former beauty queen.

"No one lives there," she said.

"Yeah, I figured. Say, did you hear anything odd tonight?"

"Odd? Like what?"

"Like screaming or banging noises."

"No...but come to think of it, my television might have been a bit loud earlier. And I *was* watching a scary movie with lots of screaming in it. Don't tell me you got sent on a wild goose chase 'cause of that?" she said with more than a hint of flirtatiousness.

"Sounds like it, ma'am. Thanks for your help."

"Anytime, officer," she said with a wink.

"Detective."

"Huh?"

"I'm Detective Brodsky."

"Well, either way, I sure am sorry you came all this way for nothing. I'll try to keep the TV down in the future."

"Thank you."

Brodsky continued his trek down the sidewalk and turned toward the other side of the building to give Anna an update.

He softened the impact of his knock to prevent frightening her and said, "Detective Brodsky," to help put her even more at ease.

She opened the door, and he was struck by her attractiveness. Unlike her neighbor, she wasn't the type of woman who would have ever participated in a beauty pageant. But in his opinion, her tall, curvaceous body and pretty face were a winning combination.

"Is everything all right, officer?"

"Detective. Mind if I come in for a minute?"

"Yes, I mean no, of course not." Her fingers struggled with the screen door's lock. After what seemed to her like an eternity, the door finally clicked open and she invited Brodsky inside.

He took in his surroundings as she motioned toward a chair and asked if he'd like to sit down. Happy to be back off his feet again, Brodsky filled her in on the past few minutes.

"So, you see ma'am, it sounds like the entire thing was nothing more than a little mix-up caused by a very loud TV."

"But how could that be? I *felt* something hit the wall."

Even as the words left her lips, her confidence in her version of events started to wane.

"These things happen a lot, ma'am. Especially in older communities like this. You see, the sounds vibrate down the walls from one unit to another, and it all ends up becoming distorted. Something that seems like it's from next door could actually be coming from two units away. As to the banging sound, that's not unusual when someone's TV or radio is sitting directly on the wall."

A voice deep inside her screamed out that his assessment wasn't correct, but she couldn't bring herself to say anything. Besides which, another inner voice had already begun picking her memories apart and telling her how dumb she'd been to call the police over nothing.

"I'm really sorry," she said quietly.

He heard true remorse and knew she had probably already started mentally self-flagellating herself over her confusion. There was no reason to rub salt into the wounds by reading her the riot act, even though that's what many of his fellow detectives would have done to prevent further issues.

"It's okay, Anna," he said in a kind tone. "Is it okay for me to call you Anna?"

She nodded and tried to hold back tears of frustration. She knew what she'd heard, and it wasn't a TV or some scream queen from a scary movie. It had been real and scary as hell.

Her inner critic piped up again. *Are you sure?*

"It's normal for something like that to be scary after what you went through the other day, Anna. No harm, no foul, okay?"

"Okay." She attempted to smile at him, but it came out as more of a grimace.

"I suggest you keep your doors and windows locked. And you might want to lay off books like that for a while," he pointed toward the paperback on her coffee table.

Embarrassed, she murmured "yes, Detective," finally getting his title right.

He smiled at the proper recognition. He'd never been able to figure out why so many people got it wrong in the first place, but it always bugged him.

"You have a good night, Anna."

"Thank you," she said and closed the door behind him. She glanced at her book and a sense of shame washed over her frame. Had she really been so influenced by the climactic chapter that she'd heard TV noises as a threat?

Tux, her black and white cat, lazily walked by and rubbed against her legs. It was a small gesture of affection – most likely prompted by a desire for more food – but it made her feel better nonetheless.

CHAPTER SEVEN

Anna's phone woke her from a fitful sleep. She saw her sister's name, groaned, then pressed the answer button.

"Hello?" she said through a haze of sleepiness.

"Anna? Did you hear?" Liz said excitedly.

"Hear what?"

"My lord, woman. Turn on the local news. Quick!"

Anna pressed the remote control with fingers that barely felt up to cooperating and realized her entire body ached.

Great. It's going to be one of those days.

As the TV roared to life, she was greeted by footage of Ford Road.

"Police haven't released the victim's name yet, but this killing does seem to be eerily similar to the two others that have already taken place here in Canton.

"Officers didn't find the body until this morning, but the time of death has been reported as sometime yesterday evening.

39

According to an earlier press conference, authorities believe the murder happened elsewhere and the body was dumped here behind this restaurant," the reporter gestured toward a building behind her.

"Do we have a serial killer on our hands? It's too early to tell, but we'll keep you posted about any updates. If you have information about these brutal murders, please contact the Canton Police Department or the Michigan State Police. Reporting live, I'm Diane Douglas, and this is Channel 7 News."

"It's just like the other killings. Her head is gone!" Liz said.

Yesterday evening? The body was moved?

"Listen, Liz, I've got to go. But thanks for letting me know."

"Wait..."

"Bye." Anna hung up.

Did I hear a murder? And if so, how come Brodsky didn't find anything?

* * * * *

Later that afternoon, the sun decided to take a break from its constant punishment of Southeastern Michigan by napping behind dark storm clouds. Before the rain could roll in, Anna picked up two trash bags and rushed them out to the dumpster. She hated taking this walk at night, and therefore almost always waited until daylight, even if that meant keeping the stinky trash inside longer than necessary.

The blacktop beneath her sandal-covered feet had several cracks and potholes. In other words, it fit in perfectly with the rest of Michigan's paved surfaces. If someone were playing a game of 'step on a crack, break your mother's back,' they'd almost certainly lose many times over before completing the three-minute trek from her front door to the closest dumpster.

"Anna!" her neighbor Rene called out happily as she came around the dumpster enclosure. Rene's feet stopped short, and the woman's striking face burst into a smile that reached her blue eyes.

"Hi, Rene."

"I heard I gave you quite a fright last night. I'm so sorry!"

"Oh, it's okay," Anna said with a hint of shame. "I'm just sorry I disturbed the detective."

"Yeah, but let's be honest; any reason is a good reason to get a hunk like him to come over, am I right?"

Anna hadn't given it much thought, but she responded in the way that seemed most socially acceptable at the moment.

"Yeah."

"So, what exactly happened?" Rene asked as the clouds started to leak. "Oh, dear! Here comes the rain. Let's head inside!"

Before Anna had a chance to consider any alternatives, she found herself jogging lightly next to Rene, who then invited herself inside Anna's home.

"Um, do you want something to drink?" Anna offered.

"Yes! Do you have any green tea?"

"Sure, I'll put the kettle on."

The two women did little more than make small talk about the weather and other innocuous topics while the water heated up, but things changed after they sat down with a warm mug of tea in their hands.

"Like I was asking earlier," Rene began, "what happened? Why did you call the police?"

"I heard a lot of screaming and my wall was vibrating a lot, too. I thought maybe someone was getting hurt."

"Okay, fair enough. But is that really all there is to it?"

Anna liked her neighbor well enough to have had several short conversations with her during the past few months. They'd even gotten together for dinner once. But she'd never shared anything truly personal or meaningful. Of course, that was par for the course with the minimal friendships she had. Maybe it was time to open up to someone?

"A few days ago, I had a really weird experience. I guess I've been on edge ever since."

Rene didn't say anything, but her enraptured face urged Anna to continue telling her story, so that's exactly what Anna did. Rene's eyes grew wide in all the appropriate spots. By the end, concern for Anna's well-being radiated off of her.

"Wow, that's really intense, Anna. I'm so sorry that happened to you," she said while placing her hand on top of Anna's right shoulder. "If something like that ever happens again, let me know. I'll be happy to help out."

"Thank you," Anna said. "That's very kind."

"What are neighbors for, right? Oh, and I promise to keep the sound down the next time I watch a scary movie," she laughed.

Anna joined in, although her laugh was half-hearted. She'd been contemplating saying something else for several minutes and decided to roll the dice.

"The thing that's really getting to me..." Thinking better of it, Anna attempted to stop.

Rene's ears perked up. She sensed a good story. "Yes?"

"You know what? Never mind. It's silly."

"Don't say that! I'm sure it's not silly. Now come on, what was it?" Rene prompted her.

"Okay...look, you've got to keep this between us, okay?"

"Of course!"

"Promise?"

"Cross my heart and hope to die," Rene said with a hint of jocularity.

"Have you heard about the recent murders?"

An excited twinkle lit up Rene's eyes. "Ooh, do you mean the serial killer?"

"That's what they're saying, yeah." *Why are people so interested in serial killers?* Anna mused.

"What about them?"

"I've been wondering if maybe...no, seriously, it's crazy. Forget it."

"No way! You made me promise and everything," Rene pretended to pout. "Now out with it! Spill your guts, neighbor."

Anna chewed on her right pointer fingernail nervously for a few more seconds before giving back in to the urge to tell someone her thoughts.

"Well, you know how the news said the body was moved to the drop site? And how the estimated time of death was between six and eight? I know you were watching a horror movie and all, but what if, you know?"

Rene's eyes showed incomprehension. "What if what, Anna?"

"What if...I heard the killer," Anna rushed through the last few words so quickly that it took Rene a beat to make any sense out of them.

"Wait, what? You think you might have *heard* the killer?"

"It's possible, right? I mean, anything is possible," Anna said, mortified by how red her cheeks were getting.

"Of course, but Anna...I mean, let's think this through more carefully. I didn't hear anything. No one else reported hearing anything. Do you see what I'm saying?"

Anna's voice took on a downtrodden tone. "Yeah. You're probably right."

"I know you had a scary encounter the other day, but try not to let it get to you too much, okay?"

"I'll try," Anna mumbled.

"That couple you saw sure does sound creepy, though," Rene said. "If anyone around here is crazy enough to go cut people's heads off, it's got to be nutjobs like that. Say...you don't think they were trying to...?"

Rene's eyes made it clear that her next thought was the stuff of nightmares.

"Trying to do what?"

"You know..."

When Anna still didn't fill in the blanks, Rene made a cutting motion across her neck with her left pointer finger.

Oh my god.

"You think they were trying to kill me?" Anna responded with a higher-pitched voice than before. Her breathing sped up as she waited for Rene's next set of words.

"Maybe? Look, I'm sorry. I shouldn't have said anything. I'm sure the police were right and they were just looking for a place to rob. It's probably nothing more than a coincidence."

Rene drained the last of her tea and sat the black mug down with a clink. "I didn't mean to upset you, Anna. I should just go. I'll see myself out." She approached the apartment's exit door and pulled it open before looking back at Anna. "I meant what I said earlier, though. If you need anything, or if anything else weird happens, I'm here."

"Thanks," Anna said thinly. Her body was still present, but she'd mentally drifted far away into the land of catastrophizing.

Could they really be killers? And was I supposed to be their next victim?

Anna spent the next few minutes worrying not for herself, but for the two women who had died since her encounter with the creepy duo. If they had been targeting her, one or both of those women could have been taken in her place. The only thing more awful than contemplating whether or not the odd strangers had planned to kill her was the thought that getting away might have doomed someone else to die.

CHAPTER EIGHT

Detective Brodsky exhaled the last puff of his cigarette. He knew his girlfriend would scream bloody murder if she caught him smoking, but tough cases made it difficult to stay off tobacco permanently. His charismatic face – with its trademark square chin, angular jaw, and piercing brown eyes – showed signs of fatigue.

He'd worked his way up from the traffic beat. The day he'd officially become a homicide detective was among the proudest of his career. But when cases like this one came up – which were about as rare as a blue moon in the more affluent part of Metro Detroit – he sometimes missed his less complicated life as a traffic cop.

There were now three dead women, and they'd all been dumped within his jurisdiction. The closest he'd come to a viable lead was the odd experience that Anna woman from the Hollows had reported, but he'd been questioning her credibility since the horror movie fiasco. And besides, even if she *had* spotted the killer, she hadn't given them enough details to be able to track the couple down. Not that they hadn't tried, mind you. But with the department stretched so thin, the best they'd been able to do was put out a BOLO, which hadn't turned up anything yet.

"What's going on, boss?" Detective Jones asked him.

Jones was younger and less experienced, but Brodsky enjoyed working with him. At first, their partnership was intended to be nothing more than a training period. By the end of their two weeks together, though, Brodsky had filed a request to keep Jones as his partner. The younger man still referred to him as 'boss' sometimes, which Brodsky took as a sign of deference to his higher seniority.

"Nothing," Brodsky said with a bitter tinge.

"Does Susie know you're still smoking?"

"Nope. So, how about you and I keep that to ourselves, yeah?"

"Of course, boss," Jones said. "Hey, do you want to grab a cup of coffee? I'm dying for a fix of *my* addiction."

"Sure, but let's just go grab it at the Biggby down the street and come right back. I want to review the case files again."

Within fifteen minutes, the legal duo was back at their desks, sucking down coffee and munching on muffins. The three case files were splayed open, and a nearby crime board contained photos of the victims.

"What do you see so far?" Brodsky quizzed Jones.

"Well, our vics are all female, and they've got similar features."

"And?"

"They were all dumped somewhere after being killed and having their heads cut off. The lab geeks say the heads came off after the women died from an injectable barbiturate overdose. Oh, and there's no signs of sexual assault."

"So..." Brodsky prompted him.

"It really looks like we're dealing with a serial killer here. And it also looks like he's not into the typical torture shit. At least that's a plus for the vics, right?"

"Yeah," Brodsky agreed.

He hated to admit it, but being shot full of barbiturates definitely had to be one of the best ways to be murdered. At least they wouldn't have felt much pain, if any at all. That wouldn't provide their loved ones much peace of mind, though. I mean, how do you tell someone, 'your wife died, but at least the bastard who did it didn't torture her first.' After all, that knowledge still doesn't bring them back from the dead.

The phone sitting on Brodsky's desk came to life at that exact second, jarring the older detective so much he almost jumped. A quick glance informed him the call was coming from dispatch, so he could dispense with the formalities.

"Brodsky here," he said. His eyes grew wide as the person on the other end told him about his next case. "We'll be right there."

He sighed, looked down, and pinched the bridge of his nose in an attempt to steady his adrenaline. Although this centering technique made time seem to slow down on his end, it was actually so quick that most people wouldn't have even noticed it.

"We've got another one," Brodsky announced to his partner as he picked up his keys. "Let's roll."

* * * * *

A bright yellow tent had been erected to protect the crime scene. This could only mean one thing: something different had happened, and the Police Chief didn't want the media to find out. Brodsky and Jones braced themselves for whatever new atrocity awaited them before flashing their IDs and walking through the colorful barrier.

"What have we got?" Brodsky asked a member of the forensics team. He took great pains to breathe through his mouth instead of his nose. This was a necessary skill for anyone who worked homicide, although it still didn't block out all of the mephitic stench associated with death.

Jane took a beat to compose herself; like many of the women in the department, she had a bit of a crush on Brodsky.

"It's another murder, but the MO has changed."

"How so?" interjected Jones.

"First off, this vic is male. Secondly, the head is still attached, but he's missing another body part."

She motioned toward the body at the center of all the commotion. Both detectives took in a deep breath at the latest mutilation.

"We've got to get Kate on this, boss," Jones opined.

"Way ahead of you, kid," Brodsky answered while looking through his phone's contact list.

"Hello?"

"Hi, Kate. It's Brodsky."

"Why, hello! I take it you have a new case for me? Or is this a personal ca..." Kate said.

"It's a case, all right," he interrupted her. His face flushed with memories of their past romance. Jones pretended not to notice, but it had become abundantly clear that Brodsky still held a bit of a torch for his ex.

"Let me guess. The serial killer struck again, and this time, the pattern has changed, right?"

Damn, she's good. How does she always know?

"Yeah, you hit the nail on the head. Like usual. How fast can you be here?"

"I'm in Detroit right now, and I need to wrap something else up first. Give me an hour."

"I'll text you the address."

CHAPTER NINE

"I'm starting to get worried, sis," Liz said into her phone. "I mean, I know I was busting your chops the other day about that odd couple you saw, but who knows, right? And how crazy is it that there's been a fourth murder so soon?"

Anna wasn't really sure what time had to do with it. The killings still would have been crazy regardless of the amount of time that passed between them. But she did appreciate her sister's concern.

"My new locks are installed, thankfully."

"And you're staying inside after dark, right?"

"Of course," Anna said. "Truthfully, I haven't stepped outside in a couple of days. Between the constant heat and humidity, my joints and muscles have been very unhappy. Add the stress of a local serial killer into the mix, and it's a wonder that I'm not in a full-fledged flare-up."

Anna expected Liz to scoff at her fibromyalgia symptoms again, but her sister allowed the opportunity to pass without comment.

"Anyway," Anna continued, "the entire community seems to be on high alert at the moment. At least that's the impression I got from the Corvo Hollows board on Nextdoor."

"Have I ever told you how weird I think your apartment community's name is?" Liz asked.

"At least a hundred times."

"I stand by my previous comments, then."

"Well, it could be worse. At least it's not Burnt Porcupine like that town we drove past in Maine," Anna laughed.

"You've got me there," Liz conceded.

As soon as the two hung up, Anna cracked the living room mini blinds open and peered out at the neighborhood. Nothing seemed amiss. In fact, the condos across the street appeared almost empty due to the shockingly low level of outside activity. She also checked every lock on the front door to make sure none of them had magically become unlatched. This had turned into an hourly ritual since the news broke about a fourth victim.

Back in her studio, she attempted to complete a project she'd started a couple of days ago. The correct shading eluded her so far, and she'd grown frustrated with her efforts. If it didn't work out soon, she'd have to scrap the entire thing and start over.

Art was the love of her life, but that didn't mean their relationship was always smooth sailing. Her digital pencil often flowed with such grace and indecisiveness that it seemed like the art was channeling her, instead of the other way around. Sometimes, though, she had to force herself to work through mental barriers that left her feeling detached from her drawings.

Even those pieces typically did well with publishers and readers, but they didn't give her nearly the same level of personal satisfaction.

Her fingers, palms, and shoulders ached, but that was nothing new. When she first began having these symptoms, she'd shut down her art for a day or two. Now, she typically persevered unless it was a particularly bad day.

Her thoughts wandered to the murders, and she obsessed again over the possibility that the creepy couple were to blame. She'd been embarrassed when Detective Brodsky came out for nothing the other day, but she'd still programmed his number into her phone. She now made sure to keep her phone on her at all times, too, even if she only planned to be out of the room for a minute. She'd rather end up labeled 'crazy' than allow herself to become the killer's – or killers' – next victim.

CHAPTER TEN

"Hi, Kate. It's good to see you," Detective Jones said while shaking the expert criminal profiler's hand.

Whatever had existed between Kate and Brodsky took place long before he made his way to homicide, but Jones could definitely understand what his partner had seen in her. Kate had a medium-brown complexion framed by long dark brown hair, along with enticing hazel eyes, a petite frame, and a smile that could outshine the sun. Top that off with a killer intellect – pun intended – and he couldn't imagine how any detective wouldn't be attracted to her.

"It's good to see you, too, Jones," she said.

Kate appraised Jones in return. She took in his tall, lanky body, black hair, and slightly large nose. Despite being in his 30s, Jones still had a boyish appearance. Combined with his last name, this had earned him the nickname 'Jughead' and also undoubtedly made it harder to be taken seriously on the job. Unless that youthful charm was actually his secret weapon. She could see it having deadly accuracy on the right female profile.

"Hey," Brodsky said as Kate moved in for a hug. She attempted to embrace him warmly, but Brodsky countered with a stiff, one-armed response.

"Hey you," Kate whispered in his ear, seemingly oblivious about his lack of enthusiasm. A heartbeat later, her body language and tone became all business. "Show me the latest body."

* * * * *

"What can you tell us?" Brodsky asked with a sense of urgency.

"I've examined the fourth vic and reviewed the case files for the first three," Kate informed the two detectives. "I'll need some time to write up a full profile, but I have several immediate takeaways."

Jones reached for a pen and pad of paper.

"You ready, newbie?" Kate joked.

Jones nodded solemnly.

"Okay, here goes. Number one: you can most likely rule out the idea of the latest vic being unrelated to the first three cases. Although the MO has changed, this doesn't look like a new killer or some type of copycat. This is what evolving looks like, gentlemen.

"Number two: I believe we're looking at the handiwork of two people working in tandem. It could be a couple, sort of like a modern day, serial killing version of Bonnie and Clyde. If not, it's probably family members. My guess would be brothers."

Brodsky and Jones shared a look with so much meaning that their thoughts could almost be plucked out of the air. If a couple had started chopping up bodies, then the odds had greatly increased that the woman from Corvo Hollows had actually seen them.

"Aside from that, all the evidence points toward two white males or a white male and white female. They're probably in their mid-30s to mid-50s, but one of them might be older.

"The lack of post-death torture suggests these are murders of opportunity, as opposed to targeted kills. The ragged, imprecise nature of their cuts indicates they have no surgical experience, or even much in the way of kitchen cutting skills. I'd peg them at average intelligence, but I'd bet one of them is charming enough to disarm potential victims."

The detectives shared another silent exchange. Kate said, "What's on your minds, gentlemen?"

Brodsky took the lead, as usual. "There's a woman who lives nearby, in the Hollows. She had an odd encounter with a couple after we found the first body. It sounded like a botched attempted at a burglary, but now I'm not so sure...the only thing, though, is they don't sound like they were very charming."

Kate shrugged. "You know these profiles are merely a guide and aren't always one-hundred percent accurate. I'd go talk to her again, if I were you. And take a sketch artist with you."

CHAPTER ELEVEN

"What's up, boss?" Jones asked.

"I'm guessing Anna is a bit too jumpy for us to just drop by, so I'm checking the caller ID for her phone number."

"Anna? That's the lady from the Hollows, right? You two on a first name basis now?" he teased.

"I've been over there twice, you know," Brodsky grunted. "Ah, here it is!"

The older detective punched in the appropriate sequence of numbers and waited for Anna to pick up.

"H-hello?" Anna said hesitantly, as if she'd never answered a phone before.

"Hi, Anna? This is Detective Brodsky. Do you have a minute?"

"Oh, hi Detective. Sure."

"My partner and I would like to come by and ask you a few more questions. Would that be okay?"

"Yes."

"We're also planning to bring our department's sketch artist with us. Do you think you can remember enough about the couple you saw to help him make a couple of sketches?"

"Sure, no problem."

Sketches! Why didn't I think of that?

"Great. We can come by in two hours, if you'll be there."

"I'll be here," she managed to reply without laughing at the absurdity of her going anywhere with a very active killer on the loose.

* * * * *

"Let's start with the man you saw," the sketch artist said to Anna.

"He was tall, mostly skinny but with a bit of a belly, and long, scraggly gray hair."

As the artist, Steve, worked on his drawing, inspiration hit.

"Hey, have you ever seen *True Blood?*" Anna asked.

"Yeah, a few times," Steve responded.

"He reminded me a lot of Joe Lee. You know, the guy who was Sam's brother's dad? He had a similar look and vibe."

Steve stopped drawing and cocked his head to the side while sorting through his memories. A smile cracked his typically taciturn exterior as he landed on the correct face. He quickly returned to his sketch with renewed gusto.

Much faster than she would have expected, Steve gently blew some loose pencil shavings off his notepad and presented it to her for approval.

"Wow," she whispered. "That's him, all right."

A hard lump formed in her throat, and no matter how many times she swallowed, it wouldn't go away. Even though the creepy man was nowhere near her right now, simply seeing his face again renewed her deep sense of fear and insecurity.

Having noticed her emotional shift, Brodsky asked, "Are you doing okay, Anna? We can take a break, if you'd like."

The offer was tempting, but more than anything, Anna just wanted to get this over with.

"No thank you."

After repeating the process with the female suspect – which was met with the same artistic precision from Steve, followed by Anna's resulting emotional response – the two detectives decided to give Anna some much-needed space.

"Thank you," she said wearily to Brodsky.

"No, thank *you* for your cooperation. These sketches are really helpful. You did a good job."

A hint of unprofessional trouble lingered in the air. Brodsky cleared his throat and said goodbye.

Careful, Brodsky mentally chided himself.

The detective had a girlfriend, but things hadn't been going well with Susie for a few months. Brodsky had never been the type to cheat, but he did have to remain very aware of his boundaries.

His attraction to Anna wasn't something he intended to pursue. He'd more than learned his lesson the last time he combined work with pleasure. Seeing Kate was beyond awkward now. Plus, their relationship had been frowned upon by the higher-ups. Getting involved with a colleague was bad enough; he'd probably get fired for dating a witness.

Even if none of those things were a factor, he was pretty sure his interest wasn't mutual.

CHAPTER TWELVE

Anna sat fidgeting in the green chair she always used during therapy. Under normal circumstances, she probably would have skipped this session. Despite her concerns about going out into the world with a killer on the loose, she realized she'd never needed professional support more than right now.

"There have been four deaths. Three since I saw Mr. Weird Hair and his creepy...partner, or whatever she is. And I swear to you, Jeani, I heard noises that could only come from a murder."

"Our fears often make our experiences seem bigger than life. It's perfectly understandable for the sounds of a violent movie to have felt bigger, louder, and more realistic than usual in the wake of your scary encounter, not to mention all the recent news stories."

"Maybe..." Anna said, although she knew in her heart what she'd heard hadn't come from a television.

"You took a brave step by informing the police, and you can be proud of that. It's always better to try to help than to ignore the pleas of someone in need. But as you learned from that couple, it's also critical to always put your own safety first. You've got to attach your own oxygen mask first, you know?"

Anna nodded, but avoided eye contact.

"How have you been handling things for the past few days? Any nightmares?"

"Sleep hasn't been very friendly, but no nightmares. I've basically just locked myself in the apartment and stayed there until today."

"That's an avoidance technique masquerading as a coping mechanism, but it's perfectly understandable in light of everything. Don't forget to take care of yourself, though. That includes running errands and exercising. You know that staying cooped up in your house for too long isn't good for you."

That had been Jeani's theory ever since Anna's first visit, but Anna still didn't quite buy into it. And in this particular instance, she didn't see it as good advice, either. To her way of thinking, it made zero sense to purposefully expose yourself to a potential attack from serial killers. No, being a hermit definitely seemed like the smartest play right now.

"Anna? Are you still with me?"

Anna snapped back into the moment with the realization that she'd spaced out momentarily.

"Yes," she confirmed.

"Good," Jeani said with a slight smile. "So, what do you think? Can you commit to taking care of yourself by not staying inside every day?"

"Sure," Anna answered half-heartedly.

Jeani appeared to accept Anna's single word reply, even though she had no real intention of following through with it. Sometimes, she found herself wondering just how good of a judge of character her therapist actually was. Shouldn't she have seen right through her lies and called her on her bullshit? Or was this what they meant by 'letting the client take the lead?'

* * * * *

As much as Anna really didn't want to take her therapist's advice, she also needed to pick up some groceries. She found herself wandering the aisles of a local Kroger after her session. She cursed herself for not having enough foresight to have placed an online pickup order instead.

Maneuvering between the other shoppers gave her anxiety, especially when they parked their cart in the middle of the aisle for no apparent reason. The ridiculously loud music and bright lights didn't help, either. Sensory sensitivities were yet another unfortunate side effect of her medical condition, and they often made it hellish to shop.

She turned her tiny shopping cart out of the pasta aisle and went in pursuit of cat food. Out of the corner of her eye, she caught the movement of a frame and face that seemed familiar.

Is that...?

Before she could get a good enough look, another shopper's cart collided with hers.

"Excuse *you*," the disgruntled elderly woman barked at her.

"I'm terribly sorry, ma'am," Anna said.

The white-haired woman harrumphed with such force that it shook the glasses on her face. "I should think so. Now, are you going to move out of the way or are you waiting for an invitation?"

Anna backed her cart away from the angry shopper and fought back the urge to cry. She was fairly certain she hadn't actually done anything wrong, but getting yelled at always brought up latent insecurities that were buried in a very shallow grave.

The negative encounter made her forget all about the person she thought she'd spotted out of the corner of her eye. Surveying the parking lot as she headed toward her car brought it all crashing back, though. There was a small black pickup truck parked two spots away from hers.

Is that them? Should I call the police?

Sweat broke out across her body while she finagled her grocery bags into the blue Saturn's trunk.

Maybe I should wait to see if it's really them?

This thought was immediately squashed by a more prevalent one.

Eff that! I'm out of here.

She drove away, but not before selecting the detective's name from her contact list.

"Detective Brodsky. How can I help?"

"Detective? It's Anna Collins. I think I just saw them again."

"Slow down, Anna. Where did you see them?"

"I'm pretty sure that at least the guy is at the Kroger on Canton Center Road right now. I only saw him out of the corner of my eye, but a truck just like theirs is in the parking lot, too."

"Thanks for the tip. We'll check it out," he said hurriedly and hung up before Anna could respond.

CHAPTER THIRTEEN

Brodsky and Jones performed a quick check of the packed parking lot upon arriving, but no small black pickup truck stood out to them. On the offhand chance they'd missed it, the duo headed inside to canvass the store. This type of procedure needed to be handled delicately; if they made the wrong move, shoppers would get panicked. The good news was that they were both wearing suits instead of police uniforms.

The two split up to cover ground more quickly. They knew every passing second made it less likely they'd find the attempted B&E suspects – who also might be killers.

Brodsky took each aisle turn carefully and attempted to blend in. To that end, he picked up a handcart and a few random items. Navigating around the customers wasn't easy. An elderly lady with white hair made things particularly difficult as she moseyed along. The way she held up everyone else almost felt intentional, but it wasn't illegal to be an aisle hog.

Jones and Brodsky met in the center of the store and agreed that they'd missed their target. On the walk outside, a man who'd just exited the self-checkout area bumped into Brodsky's back.

"Sorry," the man muttered as he veered around the detectives.

"No problem," Brodsky said before getting a look at the tall, thin man's unruly gray hair. "Sir? Excuse me, sir?"

The man grabbed two shopping bags out of the cart before shoving it behind him. His feet pounded the pavement and his lungs burned as he approached his truck.

The detectives had their own problems to contend with as they'd been taken completely off guard by the shopping cart. The well-aimed distraction had collided with Jones, knocking him to the ground and banging up his left leg.

"Dammit!" Brodsky said as a black pickup truck veered out of the parking lot. The distance was too great for him to make out the license plate, and there wasn't much hope they could catch up with him by the time Jones limped to the department's vehicle.

Brodsky ran ahead of his partner and jumped into their car. He grabbed the CB unit's attached microphone and said, "Brodsky here. We have a BOLO for all units. We're in pursuit of a small, black pickup truck, headed south on Canton Center Road."

By the time they made it onto the road, the truck had disappeared. They spent the next hour jig-zagging around the city but came up empty. No other units on patrol spotted the truck.

"Sorry," Jones said for the fifth time when the duo decided to call it a night.

"Knock it off, Jones. It's not your fault, and I'm getting sick of telling you that."

Mildly abashed, Jones sat back and tried to relax during the five-minute drive to the station.

CHAPTER FOURTEEN

A steady stream of noises coming from the apartment behind hers informed Anna that she'd either gotten a new neighbor or had completely lost her mind. It had been about twenty-four hours since her trip to Kroger, and she hadn't heard anything from the detectives. Nothing was on the news, either, so she assumed they hadn't caught up with the couple.

She'd started to doubt her recollection of events. Had he been in the grocery store? Had she ever actually seen them at all? Could it have been nothing more than a bad dream?

Interestingly, the killings had seemingly stopped, too. It had been a few days now since the fourth victim was discovered, and she hoped that would be the end of it.

Her door vibrated under the pressure of someone knocking from the other side. After a moment's hesitation, she moved forward and opened the door.

"Hi, neighbor!" Rene said. The screen door had muted her words, but it was easy enough to decipher the message.

"Hi, Rene. Come on in."

Once both doors were shut and locked up as tight as Fort Knox, Anna turned to Rene. "What's going on?"

"Did you see we've got new neighbors?"

"Behind me?"

"Yeah, next door to me. They seem a bit odd, but they're friendly."

Anna knew Rene would have collected more information than she'd initially shared. Rene was nice, but she also tended to root out even the smallest scraps of gossip. Finding out the basic details about our new neighbors definitely fit into this category.

"What else did you find out?"

"Let's see," Rene said, relishing her role as the keeper of neighborhood information. "They're an older couple, probably both at least in their fifties, but he's clearly the oldest. His head is as bald as a cue ball," she laughed, although not mean-spiritedly.

"They moved up here from Tennessee and definitely have the accents to prove it. The woman might be having some type of mid-life crisis because she looks like a teenaged Goth, complete with black hair and an ankh necklace."

"Weird," Anna giggled, despite knowing she had no right to judge. After all, she'd been wearing the same style since high school.

"Oh, and I told them about our parking spots. They didn't seem to have any issue with taking the one that the old neighbors always used. He actually moved their truck to the right spot after I filled him in."

"Truck? What type of truck?"

"Oh, I don't know. But it's bright red, so you can't miss it!"

"Now we only have one empty apartment left in the building."

"Oh, that's right! The one next door to you is vacant, too. I wonder when you'll get a new neighbor. Hopefully, it's a hottie!" she said with a suggestive look in Anna's direction. "Speaking of hotties, I forgot to tell you! James will be home in time for Christmas!"

Rene's husband, James, was in the Navy. He'd been on active duty since before Rene moved into the Hollows three months ago.

"That's great!" Exhaustion sunk into Anna's body. One of the biggest drawbacks of socializing was that it always made her tired. She issued an exaggerated yawn, in the hopes Rene would take the hint.

"Still not sleeping well?"

"Nope. But I'm thinking about taking a nap."

"Sounds like a smart move. I'll get out of your hair, then."

Anna opened the door for Rene. "Thanks for stopping by."

"Have a nice nap," Rene said with a smile and a wink.

* * * * *

Anna's wall shook under the force of fierce pounding coming from the apartment behind hers. She jolted awake as a burning sensation ran down her right leg.

Damn neuropathy!

She had gotten used to having random burning, tingling, and pinching sensations throughout her body; they were all part of her medical condition. Her tense nerves screamed that something else had happened to wake her up, but she couldn't quite put her finger on it.

She rubbed pain-relieving balm on the angry section of her leg and the burning dissipated. Anna resided in that halfway point between wanting to fall back asleep or simply get up, so she laid her head back down on the pillow to contemplate her options. Naturally, her eyes fluttered only once before closing again.

BAM! BAM! BAM!

Her eyes shot back open, and this time she understood the source of her sudden wakefulness. The banging had returned. Angry at yet another interrupted moment of sleep, she stalked across her apartment and rapped three times on the back wall.

Her knocking was almost immediately answered by three thuds that shook the wall and floor.

"I've had enough of this crap," she muttered to herself while pulling her clothes on. Less than five minutes later, she walked purposefully around the building and knocked tersely on her neighbors' door. When that didn't get any results, she allowed her knuckles to issue a long, loud plea for attention.

"What's going on?" Rene asked as she stepped out of the unit next door.

"They're being ridiculously loud!"

"Are you sure?"

"Of course, I'm sure!" Anna shot back.

"It's just that, well, I'm pretty sure I saw them leave about an hour ago. I don't think anyone's home."

Anna stared at Rene blankly.

"Then how the hell…"

"I don't know. Maybe you dreamt it? You did take a nap, right?"

"I did, but no, I didn't dream it. I was standing right by the wall when they banged on it the last time!" Anna said indigently.

"Huh. Maybe there's something in the walls?"

"That's what the apartment manager thought. But the maintenance guy swears there's nothing in there."

"That's really weird," Rene said with a look that made Anna angry.

"I'm not imagining things, Rene. Nor am I dreaming them."

"I don't think you are, Anna," Rene said in a placating tone, but Anna picked up a hint of insincerity.

Great. She thinks I'm crazy.

"Maybe something fell against the wall a few times or something. I don't know," Anna trailed off. "I guess I'll talk to them about it later."

"Sounds good, hon. How about you go home and try to get some more sleep?" Rene said with concern.

"Good idea," Anna mumbled before walking back to her side of the building.

I don't care what she says. I know someone – or something – is over there.

CHAPTER FIFTEEN

Anna hated the neighbor at the end of her side of the building. It wasn't that he creeped her out – although he kind of did – but more that he never knew when to shut up.

"Don…" she tried to interject, but he bowled right over her.

"I can't believe it happened again! We've had more murders in town over the past few weeks than we've ever had. It's crazy. I hope you're taking extra precautions, Anna."

Don looked at her expectedly from his tiny eyes that were practically hidden beneath the oversized, 80s-style glasses covering half of his wrinkly face. His thinning, grayish-black hair stood askew, as always. She would have bet good money on her guess that his hair hadn't seen a brush or comb in decades.

"Yes, of course. Look, I've got to go," she managed to get out without being interrupted.

Two sentences in a row? Must be a world record.

"Be careful," he urged her.

"I'm just going to the mailbox to pick up a package, Don," she said with a bit more snark than intended.

Don recoiled slightly. This was the one topic that could almost always get him to stop bugging her. Back when she'd first moved in, he'd vastly overstepped her boundaries by signing for one of her packages, which he then kept in his home for several hours.

She'd been livid when the UPS representative told her what Don had done, especially since she'd been home at the time of the delivery. The discussion they'd had later that day when she retrieved her package made it clear she didn't want him to do that again. Fortunately, that was one of the rare times when he'd actually taken a few seconds to listen instead of rambling on endlessly.

She saw her opportunity to leave and took it.

"See you later, Don."

He slinked back into his apartment – most likely to pout about her unwillingness to humor him any longer. Anna hated to come off as rude, but some people never took the hint without a bit of brusqueness.

Her mail key fit roughly into the box – like usual – and she had to fight with it to get the door open. Her efforts were met by a vast, empty darkness. Disappointed, she relocked the box, stepped back, and saw a small red pickup truck headed in her direction.

Everyone in this community had a bad habit of driving too fast, and her new neighbors seemed to be no exception. Anna hastily retreated to the grass next to the mailboxes and waited for the vehicle to pass.

That looks exactly like...

It was a dead ringer for the black pickup truck from several days ago. Aside from being red, that is. Fascinated and slightly repulsed, she retracted her steps across the cracked blacktop while keeping a close eye on the truck's occupants.

Two people stepped free of the vehicle, and their frames made her freeze in place.

It couldn't be. Right?

Although the man was bald and the woman sported a jet-black hairdo, she could have sworn they each had the exact same height and build as the oddest couple she'd ever encountered.

Could it be? And what if they're the killers?

* * * * *

Anna stayed in for the rest of the evening and spent the night tossing and turning. She finally gave up on the idea of sleep when an insistent weed-whacker turned its vengeful attitude on the stubborn weeds and grasses hiding against her exterior wall.

Her first coherent thought centered around Don's statement from yesterday: "I can't believe it happened again!" This potentially important detail had slipped free of her grasp last night as she'd ruminated on the odds that her new neighbors were the mystery couple.

The cold light of the television lit up her bedroom as she searched for more information. It didn't take long to discover that the story had captured nationwide attention.

"With the death count currently sitting at five, police in Canton and throughout all of Metro Detroit are scouring the area to find clues. Although Canton Chief of Police Chet Brower hasn't said the words yet, it's become abundantly clear that a serial killer is stalking the streets of this formerly quiet suburb. Let's go to my special in-studio guest, Dr. Brad Fenwick. Dr. Fenwick is the nation's premiere expert on serial killer pathology."

"Hi Anderson," Fenwick said. His soft brown eyes exuded warmth, and the combination of his suit, immaculately tailored white beard, and relaxed body language caught Anna's eye.

No wonder killers talk to him.

"What can you tell us about these murders, Brad? Isn't it highly unusual for a serial killer to target both genders?"

"It's not nearly as unusual as you'd think. These killers attach themselves to a certain script, but that doesn't mean it has to be played out with only one type of person. In some cases, they'll kill people of all ages and genders, with each person serving as a stand-in for a family member."

The silver-haired senior reporter's determined jawline and serious expression didn't show any changes as he launched into his next question. "Why do you think the male and female victims are being dismembered in different ways?"

"That's hard to speculate about at the current time, Anderson. Until the police release details about exactly what's been done to the male victims, I wouldn't dare to hazard a guess. But what we do know for sure is that each female victim has been beheaded, and the heads haven't been recovered. This typically signifies a killer's desire to not only silence these people but to also keep a souvenir."

"So, you're saying the killer may have actually kept the heads?"

"That's exactly what I'm saying. Now, the good news is that keeping mementos of that type will make the killer more prone to accidental discovery. It's not uncommon for an unsuspecting spouse, child, or friend to stumble upon the proof of a killer's gruesome crimes. And heads are a lot harder to keep hidden than something smaller, like a finger. In either case, steps need to be taken or the remains will also emit a telltale odor."

"Gruesome indeed," the reporter said with the perfect blend of professionalism, horror, and compassion for the victims' families. He was a pro at delivering his words through this steady, measured tone, and it had made him Anna's favorite source of national news coverage.

Anna turned the television off before it could deliver any more bad news. After completing her basic morning routine, she took refuge from the world inside her art studio. She needed to send over a few completed pieces to her current client, and this seemed like the perfect time to email them. Once everything was bundled into a zip file and sent to the publisher for approval, she powered the computer down and pulled out her iPad.

Anna wouldn't be starting a new contract for a few days. As long as the publisher didn't want any crazy, last-minute tweaks – *they'd better not,* she thought – she'd have ample time to mentally reboot for the next job. In the meantime, she could work on a couple of personal projects.

Her pencil met the screen and everything else faded away. Anna's intention had been to draw a Japanese maple tree in all its blazing red glory. Instead, she found herself wandering down a dark mental alley filled with murderers. Sighing, she allowed herself to finish the sketch as a way of purging her anxiety about the town's first active serial killer.

Hidden within the digital pencil marks and appropriately ambient shading were a few disembodied objects. She knew about the heads because practically every news channel brought them up on an hourly basis. Unsure what the other missing body parts were, she conjured up a couple of severed feet and hands, along with a few missing eyeballs.

"Ugh," she said aloud while examining the finished piece. "That's more than enough of *that* type of drawing."

Anna moved the drawing into the recycle bin. At the last second, she changed her mind and hit 'restore' on the file. Uncertain why she'd decided not to trash the disturbing image, she moved it into a folder marked "Miscellaneous."

CHAPTER SIXTEEN

Dammit!

Anna's walls were still shaking from yet another round of pounding.

That's it! I can't take it anymore!

Her feet pounded the pavement as she once again circled the building. With her interest in being polite long gone, she slammed her knuckles against the door three times.

"Just a sec!" someone shouted from inside.

Anna's heat-soaked shirt clung to her back after only two minutes outside. She had zero patience left for loud noises and was already mentally composing her complaint letter to the management office.

The front door opened, and all the air in Anna's lungs disappeared. Her head swirled with the disorienting dizziness of drinking far too much, and her skin crawled with goosebumps, despite the sun's insistent rays.

"Can I help you?"

Anna tumbled to the sidewalk and hit her head. Before the lights went out completely, she experienced a pang of fear so pronounced that it threatened to instantly freeze her blood.

I'm going to die.

* * * * *

"Miss? Can you hear me?"

A groan slipped through Anna's lips as the world came rushing back into focus. She found herself staring into the concerned eyes of an EMT.

"What happened?" she managed to whisper hoarsely.

"You fainted. It's probably just heat stroke, but I'd like to run a few quick tests with you to make sure you didn't hurt your head, okay?"

She issued half a nod before dizziness brought vomit to the back of her tongue. Seeing her eyes get hazy, the EMT reached behind her before she could fall again.

"I've got ya, Miss. It looks like you might have a concussion. I'm going to take you to the hospital now. Just hang tight while we get you situated for the ambulance ride."

"Hospital? No, I don't..."

"I have to, Miss," he interrupted. "It's procedure. Besides, you don't want to mess around with a head injury. You could have bleeding on the brain."

A new fear took over. How in the world was she supposed to pay for all of this? Yes, she had insurance, but her deductible was ridiculously high. There were many good things about working for herself, but quality insurance coverage definitely wasn't one of them. And, like many Americans, she knew there wasn't much in her savings account to make up the difference.

"Are you okay, Anna?"

Rene's voice cut through the confusion and fear, which instantly gave her an idea.

"Rene? Would you be willing to do me a huge favor?"

"Sure, what's up?"

"The EMT says I need to go to the hospital, but the ambulance ride..."

"Ah, gotcha. A bit rich for your blood, right? Mine, too. I can drive you."

"Will that work?" Anna asked the EMT.

His dark brown eyebrows scrunched up as he considered the situation, then he relented. "As long as you promise to head straight there."

"Scouts honor," Rene said.

A short drive later, they pulled up at the entrance to the closest emergency room.

"I don't think you should walk all the way from the parking lot, Anna. Go ahead and get out here. I'll catch up with you in a few minutes."

Anna gratefully exited the car. A rush of wooziness caused her to sway slightly, but she managed to get the car door shut and headed indoors. She passed through the entrance before the wooziness returned with reinforcements. The world spun out of control, and she plopped down into a wheelchair.

"I've got you!" a man's voice said proudly.

"Huh?" Anna moaned as her vision shifted in and out of focus.

"Let's get you checked in."

Flashes of the hospital made their way through her unfocused eyes, but she wouldn't have been able to recount the exact trip from the entrance to the check-in desk even if her life depended on it.

The wheelchair came to a halt, and she got her first hazy look at the helpful man. Green scrubs covered his tall, solid frame, and his dirty blond hair peaked out from underneath a baseball cap. Anna tried to tune into his conversation with the woman behind the counter.

"You're still here?"

"I was headed out when I caught a patient," he grinned. "She appears to have a head injury, probably a TBI. Let's get her checked in right away."

"There you are!" Rene said loudly as she approached the desk. "I thought I'd lost you!"

"Hi, ma'am. You're with her?" the man in scrubs asked.

"I sure am," Rene replied with a hint of flirtatious energy.

Leave it to Rene to flirt while I'm dying, Anna chuckled to herself. She regretted this action a half beat later when a wave of nausea washed over her body.

"Can you help her fill out these forms?"

"Absolutely! Anything you say, doctor."

"I'm not a doctor," he said without any hint of irritation. "I'm a nurse. And I was just on my way home. So, if you've got this...?"

"Oh, sorry! Of course, of course. Thanks for your help," Rene blurted out in one quick burst. Her embarrassment at mislabeling the man could have easily been noticed from the other side of the room.

Rene filled out as much as she could and got a few answers from Anna. With this task completed, they moved on to the hospital waiting game. Rene expressed her displeasure at the fact that Anna wasn't bumped to the head of the line, but Anna no longer had a concrete sense of time.

Almost thirty minutes later, Anna finally found herself sitting inside an examination room. No one checked on them for another twenty minutes, during which time Rene tried her best to keep Anna conscious.

"What happened, anyway?" Rene prompted her.

"I...I don't really remember."

"You were outside the new neighbor's door. They called 911."

"The new neighbors?"

"Yeah, remember? The people who you thought were being loud when they weren't actually home?"

The memory of the door opening smacked her in the face with as much force and subtly as a shovel. Her eyes widened and her hands trembled.

"Anna? Are you okay?"

"No," she managed to utter before a doctor knocked on the door.

"What seems to be the problem?" a short brown-haired woman wearing blue scrubs asked with the feigned enthusiasm of someone who has asked the same question millions of times.

"My friend passed out and hit her head. She's been having trouble walking, and I'm pretty sure she's not seeing or remembering things clearly."

"And her name is Anna?" the doctor asked.

"Yes," Anna answered weakly.

"Well, that's a good sign, at least. Let's see what we've got here, shall we?"

The doctor pulled out an ophthalmoscope, shined the light into Anna's eyes, and then checked to see if the patient could follow her pointer finger.

"Good. Now, how many fingers am I holding up?"

"Uh…" Anna blinked her eyes a couple of times. "Three?"

"That's right," the doctor smiled. "Are you experiencing any nausea?"

"Yes. And dizziness."

"That's not out of the ordinary after falling," she said while physically examining the back of her head. "You've got quite a bump here."

"Ouch!"

"Sorry about that. The bump is clearly very sensitive, too. It definitely looks like you've got a concussion, but I see no signs of anything more serious. I'm going to ask you to sit tight for a couple of hours, and we'll come in and check on you every half-an-hour or so. If nothing changes, you can go home."

"Thank you," Anna managed to say as she became cognizant of her brand-new raging headache. "You don't have to stay," she offered to Rene.

"Are you kidding? I'm staying, silly. You shouldn't be alone. Besides, how are you going to get home later?"

"I appreciate it," Anna said before her head leaned against her right shoulder and she fell asleep.

"Anna? Shit!" Rene left the room in search of help. She spotted a nurse rounding the corner and raced to catch up with her. "My friend has a concussion and she just fell asleep. What should I do?"

"Don't worry," the nurse replied kindly. "Unless the doctor said she shouldn't sleep, then it's fine."

"But I thought?"

"Outdated thinking. We haven't followed that guideline in years, but most people don't seem to know that."

"Oh. Well, thanks. Sorry I bugged you."

"It's not a bother at all," the nurse said. "I'd rather you ask a question than let something happen to your friend."

The nurse smiled at Rene again and lightly patted her shoulder as she walked past. A sense of sadness welled up in Rene's stomach as she realized that things could have been much worse. Shaking her head, she turned back toward Anna's room.

* * * * *

"Let me stay on your couch tonight," Rene said several hours later as she helped Anna get back into her apartment. The doctor had cleared her to go home but had cautioned that she should return if her symptoms worsened.

"Oh, I don't want to trouble you any further."

"It's no trouble. I just want to help. You *are* my favorite neighbor, you know."

Until that exact second, Anna hadn't known Rene viewed her that way. It was a pleasant but slightly befuddling surprise. One look at Rene told Anna there was no point in debating any further, so she gave in to Rene's offer to stay the night.

"If you need anything during the night, just call out to me, okay? Or call my cellphone if that's easier."

"Thank you, Rene. Your help means a lot to me."

"Anytime. What are friends for, right?"

CHAPTER SEVENTEEN

"Unnhhhh," Anna groaned as sunlight peaked through a tiny opening in her blackout curtains. She tried to sit up and the world tilted a few degrees to the left. A marching band had also apparently taken up residence inside her head, and the drum line insisted on pounding out a discordant beat over and over again.

She flipped on her lamp and recoiled from the light like a vampire facing the sun. Noises caught her attention from the other side of the apartment and her heart sped up.

Someone's in my apartment.

The metallic taste of panic hit her tongue. She reached for her phone and a nearby baseball bat. Before she could finalize her survival plan, someone rapped gently on her bedroom door.

"Are you awake?" Rene said, almost too quietly to be heard.

Rene!

Feeling foolish, Anna tossed the bat away before responding. "Yes. Come on in."

A delicious aroma entered the room.

"I made you some breakfast. Waffles and hash browns."

"Wow, thanks! No one has ever made me breakfast in bed before," Anna laughed before grabbing her pounding head. "Ugh. Remind me not to laugh."

"Are you doing okay?"

"I think so, but my head sure hurts like hell."

Rene nodded her understanding and sat on the bottom edge of the bed while Anna picked at her food.

"This is really tasty, Rene."

"I made it from scratch. You know, by pulling the items out of my freezer and heating them up," Rene chuckled. "I'm glad you like it."

"Like it? I *love* it. Maybe I should get a concussion more often." The joke reached Anna's eyes, but she kept herself from laughing out loud.

"Hey now, the first concussion's a freebie. After that, I've got to start charging you," Rene joked.

"By the way," Anna began. "I remember what happened. I went over there to ask them to stop being so loud because, of course, they were banging on the walls again. The person who answered is definitely the same woman who tried to get into my house a few weeks ago. It scared me half to death to lock eyes with her again."

"Are you sure? I mean, they don't really match the description you gave me before."

"I'm sure, Rene," Anna said with conviction.

"Well, then I guess we should keep an eye on them," Rene replied with more than a hint of caution and skepticism.

Rene's response frustrated Anna, but she knew better than to keep pushing it. At least for the moment, anyway.

* * * * *

A few hours later, Anna had finally succeeded in convincing Rene that she was okay to be left alone for a while. As soon as her neighbor was gone, Anna feverishly slid all the locks in place and reached for her phone. She hesitated briefly and wondered if she'd somehow made a mistake, but she knew in her heart that the new neighbors were the same people who had tried to get into her home.

"Detective Brodsky here. How can I help?"

"Detective? This is Anna Collins again," she said with slight embarrassment.

"Hi, Anna. Is everything okay?"

"Actually, no, it's not. Look, you're never going to believe this, but I got new neighbors a couple of days ago."

"Okay...that seems pretty normal..."

"No, you don't understand. It's *them!* You know, the people who tried to get into my apartment the other day? They moved in to the unit behind mine."

Brodsky sat up like a rod was jammed into his spine. He motioned for Jones and grabbed his notepad.

"Are you absolutely certain it's them?"

"One-hundred percent. The weird thing, though, is that they changed their appearance a bit."

Sagging back down into his seat, Brodsky asked, "What do you mean?"

Anna heard the slight change in his tone and knew she was losing his attention.

"I know, I know. This all sounds nuts. But it's not. I swear! He shaved his head and she dyed her hair. But it's definitely them. They even drive the same type of truck!"

"They're driving the black pickup truck?"

"Yes! I mean no...I mean, it's the same truck, but it's been painted red."

"I see," Brodsky said dubiously as he pinched the bridge of his nose.

"You don't believe me, do you?"

Brodsky's pause lasted one beat too long.

"I'm *not* making this up, Detective. Nor am I crazy."

The decisiveness in her tone made Brodsky second guess his initial assumption.

"Of course not, Anna. I don't think that. Can Detective Jones and I come by in a few minutes to discuss this in more detail?"

Relieved that she was finally being taken seriously, Anna agreed. As she hung up, she issued a plea to the universe.

Please let this be the end of it.

* * * * *

"Tell us exactly what happened, Anna," Brodsky prompted her.

With a quick look between Brodsky and Jones, who both sat in rapt attention, she launched into her tale. She explained everything that had happened during the past twenty-four hours, including how horrific it had been to make eye contact with that wretched woman again.

"Well..." Jones began. "It *is* unusual for perps to do something like this, but I guess if they were going to, it would make them feel better to change their appearance in some way."

"True," Brodsky took over. "And in such a scenario, the perps might believe that no one would recognize them. It's not the smartest idea in the world, but no one said criminals were geniuses."

Anna could see them trying almost desperately to find a way to make the pieces fit. What she couldn't figure out was if they believed her or if they were merely humoring her.

"Are you going to go talk to them?" she asked.

The officers shared a quick look, then Brodsky said, "We will, but not right away. We have to investigate the situation a bit more closely first."

"What does that even mean?" she asked with noticeable exasperation.

"We have to do our due diligence, Anna. We can't just start interrogating everyone who seems suspicious. We start by running their license plate to get a name. But don't worry, we'll have some people keeping a close eye on them in the meantime."

"Okay...that makes sense," she conceded. "But what should I do during all of this?"

"Steer clear of them," Jones said.

"Yes, it's best to stay away from them as much as possible. But at the same time, try not to do or say anything else that could bring attention to you," Brodsky concurred.

"Are you sure it's safe here?"

"Stay inside with the doors locked. Don't go out at night. And keep your phone handy at all times. Call us anytime, day or night. As a matter of fact..."

Brodsky removed a business card from his shirt pocket, flipped it over, and wrote down his cellphone number. "Here," he handed it to her. "Now you'll be able to reach me no matter what."

Gratitude lit up her face, and she promised to call if she noticed anything that felt even the slightest bit off.

* * * * *

Jones smirked at Brodsky as they climbed into their unmarked car.

"What?"

"Oh, nothing," Jones said coyly.

"Out with it," Brodsky said.

"It's just...you gave her your cellphone number, boss. Are you sure that was a wise idea? Seems like the type of thing that would upset the missus."

"First off, she's not my wife, so she's not 'the missus.' And secondly, this is work-related. She'll understand."

I hope so, anyway, he thought.

"Now let's get back to the station. And don't forget to call in a few unis to babysit the Hollows."

"I'm on it, boss."

CHAPTER EIGHTEEN

"What did you find out about the Hollows couple, Jones?"

"The vehicle is registered to a Timothy Dellmond. I ran him through the database and found a few minor hits, mostly traffic infractions. There was one reported domestic violence incident, but the charges were dropped."

"Is there another name on that report?"

"Yeah, it's Jennifer O'Neil. I ran her too. Looks like she's not too good at parking, enjoys petty theft, and has bad taste in men. She's racked up several domestic violence reports, but none of them have stuck. She did do a little time for possession. Looks like it was just a dime bag, though, so nothing that would even be illegal here anymore."

Brodsky scowled at the reminder that Michigan's citizens had opted to make recreational marijuana legal. He didn't think the crazy prison sentences that used to be handed out for marijuana were fair, but he still wasn't a big fan of what he viewed as a massive overcorrection to the system.

"It's not much to go on," Brodsky pondered. "But it does show a tendency for violence. Or being in violent situations, anyway.

Plus, a general disregard for basic laws. I'm not so sure that adds up to them becoming serial killers, though."

"That's what I thought, too. But the thing is, boss...Tennessee had an active serial killer until the murders suddenly stopped about a few months ago. Maybe it *is* them and they decided to take their show on the road?"

"Shit," Brodsky muttered. "Let's go talk to them."

* * * * *

After careful deliberation, Brodsky decided their best bet was to talk to Dellmond and O'Neil about the incident Anna had reported. That way, they wouldn't rush headfirst into any serial killer accusations, which could easily make them either lawyer up or leave town in a hurry. At the same time, he wanted to gather as much intel as possible, so his first goal was to carefully find out where the couple had been on the night of the first killing.

"Hello?" a woman who they presumed to be Jennifer O'Neil said through the screen door.

"Hi, ma'am. My name is Detective Brodsky, and this is my partner, Detective Jones. We were hoping you had time to answer a few questions?"

Red blotches spread across the woman's face almost instantly. This clear indicator of stress didn't mean much to the detectives because most people experience a surge in anxiety when the police knock on their door.

"Um, sure. What's this about?"

"There was an odd incident in the neighborhood last week, and we're just interviewing everyone about it."

"Oh. Well, I'm not sure how I can help you with that. You see, we just moved in a few days ago," she responded with a clear southern twang.

"Even still, ma'am. You'd be doing us a favor if we could talk to you for a few minutes."

Her hesitation was palpable.

Jones piped in, "It would let us cross your unit off the list is all, ma'am. The Chief is a stickler, you know?"

Somewhat charmed and mollified by Jones' psychological trick, the woman stepped outside of her apartment and carefully shut the door behind her. She pointed toward a couple of folding lawn chairs while opening one up for herself. Once everyone was seated, she asked, "So, what do you need to know?"

"Where were you on July 9th?" Brodsky asked.

She visibly bristled and a complaint sprung to the tip of her tongue. Before she could spit it out, Jones reassured her the questions were procedure only, and nothing more.

Relaxing into the lawn chair, she pushed her jet-black hair back and started fiddling with the ankh around her neck.

"Let's see...the 9th? That was...what? Last Tuesday?"

Brodsky nodded.

"I was on the way to Michigan. We left Tennessee that morning and didn't get here until the 10th."

"You're absolutely certain about those dates?"

"Sure am."

"Okay, just one more question, then. If we needed to verify your whereabouts on the 9th, would you be able to do that for us?"

"Sure can. Wait here," she said and moved toward her front door before either detective could say anything. A few minutes later, she returned with a Kentucky gas station receipt. It was dated July 9th at 1:43 p.m.

"As you can see, we were nowhere near Michigan on the 9th. We stopped a couple of hours later because my boyfriend got a terrible migraine."

"Have you noticed anything weird since moving in?"

"No? Well, nothing aside from our neighbor passing out on our front step the other day."

"Oh? What happened?" Brodsky asked with as much surprise as he could muster.

"Near as I can tell, she'd cooked her brains a bit too much in the sun. I've never understood sun worshippers myself. Give me the nighttime," she chuckled.

"Thank you very much for you time. Ms.? I'm sorry, I didn't get your name," Brodsky said.

"Jennifer. Jennifer O'Neil."

"Thank you, Ms. O'Neil. We appreciate your time."

"Good luck with whoever you're looking for, Officers."

"Detectives," Brodsky mumbled to himself as the two men retreated to their vehicle.

"What do you think, boss?"

"I think they looked damn close to the sketches. And she also admitted they got here on the day of Anna's encounter."

"But wait a minute," Jones said. "If they're also the killers, how could they have been in Kentucky at 1:43 p.m. on the day of the first murder? The body was found that morning."

"It sure was," Brodsky nodded with an odd expression.

"Wait, do you think the gas receipt was bogus?"

"Not necessarily. But how do we know if they drove two cars? Or maybe they had hired some movers."

"So...you mean, maybe the receipt was real, yet they were already in town?"

"It's a possibility, anyway."

"Then why didn't you ask her for the hotel receipt?"

"Because I don't want to spook them. Right now, I'm pretty sure she bought our story and has no idea we're really more interested in the murders. If they are our killers, then the longer they think they're in the clear, the better."

CHAPTER NINETEEN

Two Weeks Later

Anna sat in her work studio working diligently on a new commission. Her latest project was a complete one-eighty from the last job. This time, her pencils gave life to a fanciful children's book cover full of happy, smiling kids and a talking kangaroo.

She hummed absentmindedly while ensuring the kangaroo had the proper look in its eyes. She'd already learned that going too far in either direction could make the kangaroo look like anything from a deranged monster to a wide-eyed speed addict.

Although her next-door neighbors had quieted down and the news hadn't reported any new murders during the past two weeks, she still retained a bit of the edginess that had grabbed a hold of her. It almost seemed too good to be true that everything odd had stopped happening after the detectives visited her weird new neighbors one time.

Probably spooked them. I bet they're the killers.

This line of thought had kept her hyper aware. Meanwhile, the rest of the township had apparently exhaled a shared breath and went back to life as normal. The news reports on the previous victims were petering out, and there hadn't been any vigils for almost a week. Even the ever-present fundraisers and Facebook posts about 'thoughts and prayers' had mostly stopped.

Anna's sister and therapist were doing their best to shake her free of her worries. Rene hadn't gone so far as to suggest a complete return to normality, but a hint of pity crossed her face whenever the subject came up. It seemed like the whole world had moved on except for Anna.

Shaking her head at how quickly people could get past something so horrific, she put her digital pencil down, stretched her arms up toward the sky, and winced. The tension in her shoulders was worse than usual, which was really saying something.

Okay, I've got to get out of this funk.

Even with her almost constant physical pain and fatigue, Anna had always taken great solace in walking. The thought of going outside still left her on edge – not to mention her desire to avoid the blazing hot sun – so her treadmill would have to do.

Once her earbuds were in place and her workout playlist was blasting, she started on the treadmill's lowest possible setting. The sensation of walking across sand hit her legs due to the ridiculously low speed, so she cranked it up several notches. Both cats side-eyed her from the couch before settling back down for another nap.

She gradually worked up to a slow jogging pace and then lost herself in the rhythmic movement. A voice in the back of her head reminded her to take it easy, but it was often difficult to reconcile the difference between the old version of herself – which could easily walk or jog up to five miles per day – and the physical breakdown she'd experienced since being diagnosed with fibromyalgia.

Sweat poured down her back and face, but she didn't relent. Sometimes, it felt good to punish her body, even though she'd greatly regret it later when doing something as simple as walking across the room would seem almost impossible.

From the corner of her eye, she caught a quick movement on the couch. Her cats had shot up from their naps, with the youngest, Poe, literally jumping a few inches into the air. Frowning, she hit pause on her playlist and said, "What's the matter, guys?"

Their startled and quizzical expressions didn't hold any concrete answers, so she kept the sound off for a few minutes. When nothing else happened and they curled up again, Anna turned the music back on and cranked it all the way up.

Her chest tightened a bit and her leg muscles burned with exertion. Her breaths became faster, as if her lungs were trying to greedily gulp in all of the air in the room. She pondered conceding, but noticed she only needed to complete two more minutes to hit half-an-hour. With her goal set, she backed the speed down into cool off mode.

Just as her feet took their last few steps, the belt of the treadmill seemed to move from side-to-side beneath her. Anna reached for the handrails, but it was too late; she crashed to the ground as the cats ran to the back of the apartment.

As the shock wore off and her pain receptors burst into a discordant song, she carefully picked herself up, removed her earbuds, and sat on the couch. Checking herself gingerly, she spotted several new bruises and some scrapes on her arms and legs.

Figures.

She knew falling was a risk for fibromyalgia patients, but she could have sworn the treadmill caused the incident, not her body. Before she could solve this puzzle, a second odd occurrence caught her attention. A framed photograph hanging on her inner dining room wall was laying on the ground.

What the hell? Were the neighbors banging on the wall again?

Nothing noteworthy happened for the rest of the day, but the spooked look in her most skittish cat's eyes didn't disappear for hours.

CHAPTER TWENTY

"Did you notice anything strange yesterday?" Anna asked.

"Like what?" Rene responded.

"I was on the treadmill, and my cats kept acting like the apocalypse had started or something. And then I found one of my framed pictures on the floor."

"Hmmm...now that you mention it, I heard something about a semi-truck having a tire blowout on the freeway behind us yesterday. You know how stuff like that can make the entire building shake. Maybe it was strong enough to knock the photo down?"

Anna contemplated this explanation and realized it might also apply to some of the knocking sounds she'd heard. Living in an apartment that practically abutted the freeway came with a lot of road traffic noise. And sometimes, when a particularly heavy truck drove past or there was an accident, it *did* shake the walls of her home. Could she have been blaming her new neighbors for something they really didn't do?

As if reading her mind, Rene asked, "Say, you don't think that's what's been behind the knocking sounds, do you?"

"I'm..." Anna paused in a bid for more time to gather her thoughts. When no quick answers came to her, she said, "I'm not sure."

"On a different note, what are you doing tonight?"

"Nothing special," Anna replied.

"Come out with me!"

Anna groaned internally. The last thing she wanted to do was spend her night at a bar or some overly crowded restaurant.

"I don't know..."

"Oh, don't be a spoilsport! You just said you don't have anything special going on. We can go to the bar and grille at the corner. They have *fabulous* food!"

Anna picked nervously at her fingernails while trying to conjure up an acceptable excuse for saying no.

"It'll be my treat," Rene said in a tempting voice.

Screw it, Anna thought.

"Okay. What time?"

* * * * *

Three hours later, Rene and Anna took a seat at the bar. In Anna's mental appraisal, Rene had dressed in an outfit that issued a flirtatious warning to every man: "You can flirt with me and buy me drinks, but you'll still be going home alone at the end of the night."

Meanwhile, Anna had stuck with comfort over all else, like usual. Her khaki shorts, old t-shirt, and pulled back hair sent the message that she wasn't looking to entertain anyone. Or at least she hoped it did.

The barflies began to swarm around Rene before their first drinks arrived.

"Aren't you as pretty as a picture?" a balding, unattractive man in his late-40s said.

Rene's look said it all: Not interested. Move along, please.

Although Anna couldn't blame Rene for not wanting to exchange pleasantries with someone who was probably looking for nothing more than a one-night stand, she still secretly felt sorry for him. It had to be difficult to approach women like that, and even more so when good looks weren't on your side. The amount of confidence it required also impressed her, since she'd never been able to do anything similar.

When their drinks arrived, Rene suggested a toast.

"Here's to friendship, weirdos, and good food!"

Their glasses clinked off of each other as Anna chuckled at Rene's joke.

Anna sipped at her amaretto sour and briefly closed her eyes. She hardly ever drank, but when she did, she almost always chose this particular alcoholic beverage. Its combination of playful sweetness and commanding tartness danced over her tongue and slid down her throat without the pain that would have accompanied something harder such as whiskey.

Rene eyed Anna's reaction with an approving grin. "Good stuff, huh?"

"Yeah, definitely."

Small talk resumed until their meals arrived. With one look at her ridiculously large burger – which had way too many toppings – Rene's focus completely shifted from talking to eating. Anna, on the other hand, took small bites of her garden burger and salad, making sure to chew each bite thoroughly.

About halfway through their meal, another man approached the table. Rene spotted him in her peripheral vision and moaned. Before he had a chance to speak, she said, "Dude, I'm kind of in the eating zone here, okay?"

He did a double-take and laughed weakly at her interpretation of his intentions.

"Sorry to interrupt, but I was hoping you'd let me buy you a drink," he said to Anna, who almost choked on her latest sip of amaretto sour.

Rene's eyes bulged slightly in shock before she happily went back to eating.

"Do you mean me?" Anna managed to squeak out at a barely discernible volume.

"Yes," he smiled. The first thing Anna noticed was that his teeth were almost perfect, but one on the top row leaned slightly too far to the left.

When she didn't say anything else for what was either an eternity or a single heartbeat, he continued, "It's just so refreshing to see such an unassuming beauty. Look around you. There are dozens of women who spent hours trying to make themselves look sexy, but you didn't even put on any makeup, am I right?"

Embarrassed, she struggled for what to say next. The only words that came out were, "Thank you?"

He chuckled at the questioning lilt and sat next to her.

"One drink, okay? And if you want me to leave after, I will. No harm, no foul, right?"

Rene could see that Anna wanted nothing more than a way out of this situation. Instead of helping her, she subtly kicked Anna's leg and shot her a look that said, "Say yes, you fool!"

Feeling trapped between her friend and the handsome stranger, she relented and agreed to his proposal. She'd have one drink. But she already knew that would be more than enough.

* * * * *

Two hours later, Anna put down her fourth amaretto sour. The world's axis had tilted, and even her glasses couldn't make her view less blurry, but she enjoyed the pleasant warmth that filled her belly. Emboldened by liquid courage, she had placed her hand on top of the former stranger's arm. As he'd told her at the beginning, his name was Jaxon, he worked for one of the auto companies, and he loved her 'girl next door' style.

They'd talked for so long that Rene ended up tapping her fingers on the bar out of boredom. But she couldn't really begrudge her neighbor the opportunity to flirt with a hot man. The thought of Anna finally getting out of her shell enough to possibly take someone home with her would be an even bigger win.

"It's been lovely chatting with you, Anna," Jaxon said through his megawatt grin. "Can I see you again?"

Anna almost said, "how about right now?" but managed to restrain herself. They exchanged phone numbers and he kissed her on the cheek before exiting.

"Wow," Rene said. "Handsome, a good conversationalist, and he's got manners, too. Face it, honey; you just hit the jackpot."

Anna nodded in agreement as she stumbled out to Rene's car.

"Hell, if he'd come up to me instead," Rene continued, "I would have had some fun tonight."

"What about your husband, James?"

"Oh, I don't mean that I would have cheated on James. But I certainly wouldn't have turned down a night of free drinks, good conversation, and some delicious eye-candy."

"He is pretty handsome, isn't he?" Anna said in a slurred voice.

"That's the understatement of the year, hon."

CHAPTER TWENTY-ONE

Jeani beamed at Anna after hearing about her night out.

"That's wonderful, Anna! I'm so glad to hear you went out and made a new friend. Are you planning to call him?"

"I don't know," Anna said evasively as her thumbs picked at the label on her water bottle.

"You have to do what feels right, of course. But instead of looking for every possible reason not to see him again, I want you to ask yourself one simple question."

Anna glanced up and made eye contact with her therapist for the first time that day.

"Repeat after me, okay?" Jeani asked. "How did it feel to spend time with Jaxon?"

Anna repeated the words as directed, and her heart turned into a lifting balloon.

"Honestly? It felt pretty darn wonderful."

"Then there's your answer! This doesn't have to become a long-term thing. He doesn't need to be the love of your life or your soulmate. But it is okay to have some fun, and it would do you a world of good to spend less time hanging out alone in your apartment. So be sure to carefully consider your options before you say no to seeing him again."

Anna hated to admit it, but it seemed like Jeani was right. Jaxon had been witty, handsome, and not even slightly pushy. She'd have to be half-crazy to not want to spend more time with him.

By the time she arrived home thirty minutes later, Anna had made a decision. She wasn't going to call Jaxon, but if he called her to ask her on a date, she'd say yes.

* * * * *

Anna knew most men typically waited a few days to call in order to appear more aloof, but she couldn't help checking her phone every few minutes anyway. After her repeated actions began grating on her nerves, she threw herself back into her work.

At first, her distracted mind had a difficult time capturing the happy, innocent essence of the kids and their friend, a talking kangaroo. Soon, though, she'd slipped back into her natural artistic skin and became so invested in the characters that she almost missed it when the phone rang.

Stunned, she shook her head to clear away the fictional world while staring at her iPhone's lit up screen. The caller ID reported that Jaxon was calling, and her back instantly prickled with sweat as the pounding of her heart filled her ears. She hadn't experienced these sensations in many years and was so awestruck she didn't click the answer button until just before the call went to voicemail.

"H-Hello?" she managed to utter around the coiled spring of tension in her throat.

"Hi, Anna? This is Jaxon," he responded in a smooth and friendly tone.

He's either a lot more confident than me or much better at hiding his nervousness.

"Hi, Jaxon! How are you?"

"I'm great! And you?"

"Doing well."

"I had a lot of fun with you last night, Anna. I was hoping maybe we could do it again soon? Like, maybe tonight or tomorrow night, if you're free?"

The butterflies in her stomach threatened to burst free of her mouth with a satisfied victory yell. Instead, she reined in her sudden burst of extreme excitement by saying as plainly as possible, "Yes, that sounds nice. Tonight's a bit packed, but tomorrow night works."

She didn't actually have anything pressing to do that night, but she didn't want to appear overly eager or like some type of loser who never had any plans.

"Perfect! Meet you at the same place tomorrow at 8?"

"I'm looking forward to it," she said with a gleam in her eyes.

* * * * *

More than twenty-four hours had passed, and Anna stood staring at herself in the bathroom mirror. She'd tried on five different outfits before deciding on another 'girl next door' look since Jaxon seemed to gravitate toward that. She put on a light touch of makeup and even used some mousse in her hair for the first time in what seemed like forever.

By the time she walked into the bar and grille again, her nerves had almost gotten the better of her. The stress and excitement of going on a date had her joints aching, and she knew she'd be lucky to get through the date before succumbing to fatigue. She hoped the physical toll would be worth it.

"Anna!" Jaxon said warmly as he rose from a nearby table. The two shared a quick hug, and he pulled out a chair for her.

So far, so good, she thought, pleased that he'd chosen a table away from the bar.

They shared a few drinks while waiting for their food to arrive, and the conversation flowed just as smoothly as it had two evenings ago. Before she'd even consciously given herself permission to consider the possibility of going on another date, her heart had already jumped into the deep end of the pool. Her mother would have called her smitten.

"What do you do for a living?" Jaxon asked.

"I'm an artist," she said.

"Wow, really? What type of art?"

"All kinds, really, but I work mostly on children's book covers."

"I've never met anyone before who actually made a career out of art. That's impressive, Anna."

Her cheeks glowed red; partially due to alcohol, but mostly caused by his praise.

"And you work for an automotive company?" she asked, despite knowing that's what he'd said the other day.

"Yup. Such a Metro Detroit cliché, right? But I like it. Plus, I'm no longer on the line. The hours and pay are usually good, too."

Anna's mouth opened to reply, but the words died on her tongue as she noticed a local newscast on the TV behind Jaxon's head.

Spotting her change in mood, he asked, "what is it?" before turning around to see the breaking news story for himself.

"...Metro Detroit residents are worried tonight that their local nightmare might not be over, as previously hoped. A 26-year-old woman from Plymouth Township has gone missing. Many fear she could be the latest victim of the serial killer some have dubbed The Body Snatcher. If you have any news about her disappearance, please call the police immediately. Reporting live from Plymouth, I'm Diane Douglas."

All the color had drained out of Anna's face by the time she turned back around.

"Are you okay?" Jaxon asked.

"The killer might be back," she said in an unfocused tone.

"Yeah, I'm a bit freaked out by it, too. I mean, who knows who the guy is? Why, it could even be someone sitting in here, and we'd never know it," he shook his head.

Her bottom lip quivered and she quickly glanced around the room. Seeing her fear, Jaxon reached out for her hand.

"Hey, there's no need to be afraid. I'm not going to let anyone hurt you. Besides, I shouldn't have said such a stupid thing. I'm sure he's nowhere near here."

"You don't understand..." she began.

"What is it, Anna?"

"I...I'm pretty sure I heard one of the murders being committed."

"What?" he said with a mixture of alarm and incredulity.

She proceeded to launch into the story of everything she'd encountered since the weird couple first caught her attention. Purging herself like this to someone she barely knew wasn't typical, but each time she tried to pull the breaks, her mouth betrayed her by continuing to speak. At the end of her tale, Jaxon sat across from her with a dumbfounded countenance.

"Wow," he said softly, and she feared she'd already scared him away.

"I'm sorry, I shouldn't have unloaded all of that on you. Look, I understand that it's too much," she said while rooting in her purse. She tossed a twenty-dollar bill on the table and started to get up. "I'll just go."

"Anna, wait! Where are you going? I don't want you to leave," he implored her.

"Y-you don't? I thought..."

"No, I don't. Please sit back down. I can see how everything you've been through would be terrifying, and I can't blame you for being a bit jumpy."

He took her hands and continued to issue reassurances until she relaxed. In the back of her head, she heard Rene's voice: "Face it, honey; you just hit the jackpot."

CHAPTER TWENTY-TWO

"Dish it, sister," Liz prodded Anna. "You've gone out more in the past week than you have in a year. What's gotten into you? Or should I say who?" she giggled suggestively.

"Eww, don't be so crass, Liz. No one's gotten *into* me. I did meet a nice guy, though, and we've been spending some time together."

"Holy crap, really? That's fantastic news! Tell me everything!"

Anna explained how she'd met Jaxon and gave a brief description of their three dates since then. She also went into exacting detail about his physical appearance, including his nearly perfect smile, bright blue eyes, and medium-brown hair.

"Sounds like you're really falling for this guy. When do I get to meet him?"

"Oh, no. You're not going to do the traditional interrogation of the new boyfriend. I *like* this guy and want to keep him around. You'll scare him off for sure," she laughed.

"Come on!" Liz protested through thinly veiled laughter. "It's a tradition! It has to be done. Besides, who else is going to tell him that if he hurts you, he's dead?"

"He's coming to my place for the first time tonight, so if that goes well…"

"Ooooh! Cue the "bow-chika-wow-wow" music, am I right?"

Anna's cheeks reddened. *She's almost as bad as Rene.*

"Liz! No, you are *not* right. We're just going to have a nice evening together."

"Whatever you say, sis. But take a piece of advice from me; be sure to shave your legs before he gets there."

* * * * *

Anna and Jaxon had enjoyed a nice, homecooked meal together and were now relaxing on her couch. The cats had even removed themselves for once in honor of the special occasion.

Their bodies pressed close to each other and she inhaled the scent of his cologne. Their hands were entwined, and she could barely focus on the movie playing on her flat screen TV.

Could this be the night? she found herself wondering.

With a contented sigh, she tried to get her head out of the clouds and onto the TV so that the two of them would be able to talk about the movie later.

As she got sucked into the story, her inner dining room wall visibly vibrated under the power of three sharp banging sounds. Anna shot up quickly as ice ran down her spine.

"What is it?" Jaxon asked, looking confused.

"Didn't you hear that?"

"Hear what?"

His genuinely puzzled expression made her wonder if she'd only imagined the noise or if she'd even fallen asleep for a few seconds and dreamt it.

"I guess it was nothing. Sorry about that," she said and attempted to settle back down next to him.

They made it ten more minutes into the movie before a harsh pounding made her fear that someone would soon come barreling through the wall.

"There it is again! Do you hear that?" she practically yelled to be heard over the near-deafening noise.

"I really have no idea what you're talking about, Anna. I'm sorry," Jaxon said with a hint of pity.

"I'm not crazy, you know," she snapped with more venom than intended.

"I know," he replied in a conciliatory tone. "I don't think you're crazy. But I do wonder if maybe a lack of sleep combined with all the weird things you've dealt with lately have you so on edge that you're..." he trailed off.

"That I'm what?"

"I don't know, maybe having auditory hallucinations or something? That's a sign of sleep deprivation, you know."

She wasn't sure whether to hug him for trying to be understanding or to kick him out of her house for making her doubt her own senses. Torn, she allowed his handsome visage and soft tone to influence her decision. She made amends for her behavior and laid her head against his chest as he pulled her into an embrace.

Could it all be sleep deprivation? she wondered. A quickly growing part of her psyche hoped that Jaxon was right. It would certainly be a lot better than hearing a serial killer in action and being helpless to stop him.

* * * * *

Anna woke up the next morning glowing from Jaxon's visit. She practically leaped out of bed as Poe and Tux meowed impatiently for breakfast. Her typical aches and pains were present, but her good mood didn't give her fibromyalgia any room to bring her down.

She flipped on the coffee maker and grabbed her phone. A big smile lifted her cheeks as she saw a text from Jaxon.

"Last night was wonderful, babe. Can't wait to see you again."

The combination of his words, the kissing face emoji at the end of the text, and her fond memories of the night before practically made her squeal with excitement. Much like her very first crush all the way back in high school, she found herself floating on a cloud while sharing her stomach with an entire butterfly garden.

She quickly texted back a similar message and then turned on the TV. The red 'breaking news' banner at the bottom of the screen instantly wiped the smile off her face as she sat down in shock with her mug of coffee.

"...hopes were dashed today when the almost three-week break between killings was shattered by a gruesome discovery. Many thought the madness had ended, but The Body Snatcher has officially claimed his sixth victim. This serial killer's brazen crimes stick out due to his bizarre habit of taking at least one body part with him. Reporting live from the Plymouth-Canton border, I'm Diane Douglas."

"No, no, no," Anna muttered as she slid off the edge of her seat.

A black cloud hovering inside her brain unleashed a torrent of negativity and fear. The killer *was* back, and she had heard the pounding again last night. Pushing aside Jaxon's claims to the contrary, she fixated on the potential connection between those noises and each murder.

My neighbors are murderers.

These four words etched themselves into her mind, and she knew beyond the shadow of a doubt that they were true, no matter what anyone else said. So now, the trick was to convince the right people that she had uncovered The Body Snatcher's identity. Or more accurately, the identity of the serial killing duo.

Before she could think things all the way through, her hands had dialed Detective Brodsky's number.

"You have reached the voicemail for Detective Brodsky. I'm not at my desk at the moment, but if you leave a message, I'll get back to you as soon as possible. If this is an emergency, please hang up and call 911."

The solitary beep left her disheartened, but she decided to soldier on anyway.

"Detective? This is Anna Collins. I need to talk to you. It's about the new murder. Please call me back. Thank you."

After sitting her phone down, she pondered over whether or not it would be a good idea to use the detective's cellphone number. This *was* a pressing matter, after all. Yet at the same time, she knew he must be busy at the crime scene. Indecisiveness struck hard and left her vacillating back and forth between her options. In the end, she opted to wait a couple of hours first.

CHAPTER TWENTY-THREE

The odd couple – as she'd come to know them – walked past her living room window. In shock, she stared at them until both turned their heads and glared right back. The man licked his lips in a grotesquely suggestive manner, and the woman smiled in a way that seemed more aggressive than friendly.

Spooked by their reactions and unwilling to see their faces again, she went into her art studio. It had always been her one sanctuary from the outside world; a safe, womb-like environment where she felt free to explore and express her creativity without any fear of judgment or criticism.

To calm herself, she launched full-force back into work. Lost in the wonderful world of imagination, she had no idea how much time passed in the real world. It could have been mere minutes or the seasons could have already changed several times. By the time she looked up from her latest creation, more than three hours had passed without a callback from the detective.

As Anna battled with her initial instincts over what to do, she remembered hearing the telltale thump of a package being tossed against her door during her drawing session. She couldn't remember ordering anything, but sometimes she got a little impulsive with Amazon Prime or eBay when she couldn't sleep.

Hoping for a happy surprise, she opened her front door. Instead of a package, the decapitated body of a crow waited to greet her. She screamed and stumbled backward, struggling to shut and lock the screen door.

Once both doors were properly closed and locked, she sat on the ground in shock. *Why would someone do that?* It was horrifying. And then it hit her: someone was trying to send a message. They knew what she knew, and the not-so veiled threat seemed to imply that she'd lose her head, too, if she didn't start keeping her mouth shut.

* * * * *

Anna's phone rang almost two hours after the bird incident. She almost didn't answer when she saw Detective Brodsky's name, but she figured he'd keep calling until he got through to her.

"Hello?" she said tentatively.

"Anna? It's Detective Brodsky. I got your message. What's going on?"

A long pause emanated from Anna's side of the phone and Brodsky frowned. He'd had a very long day already, and he didn't want to play games. At the same time, he'd heard a hint of fear in her voice when she answered the phone.

"Anna? Are you still there?"

"Yes...it's just...oh, never mind. I'm sorry I called you. It's nothing."

"Why don't you let me be the judge of that?"

"Um, okay..." Anna chewed on her bottom lip. She had conflicting thoughts, and fear ruled both of them. Practically whispering, she said, "I heard those noises again last night."

"You heard what? Can you speak up, Anna?"

She cleared her throat and started again at a slightly higher volume.

"Those noises. You know, the banging sounds? I heard them again. Last night. And then the news said..."

"I see. Please, go on."

What Brodsky didn't tell Anna – and what he hoped his tone hadn't betrayed – was how frustrating her news was to him. Last night, the unis assigned to keep an eye on Timothy Dellmond and Jennifer O'Neil had somehow lost their trail. The couple had taken off at approximately seven-thirty p.m., and the unis didn't reconnect with them again until almost two hours later. By that point, the couple was back inside their apartment.

"T-today, I found a dead bird outside my door."

"I'm sorry to hear that," he said through his distracted thoughts.

"No, you don't understand. It was *put* there."

"How do you know that for sure?"

"Because it didn't have a head."

Brodsky's brain shot back into hyperdrive.

"Wait, what?" he asked. "The head's missing?"

"Yes. D-do you t-think this could be a message from the killer?"

He paused, then asked, "What time did you say you heard those noises last night?"

"I'm not one-hundred percent sure, but I think it was maybe around nine?"

Shit, he thought. *Of all the nights for the unis to fall down on the job.*

"I'm going to come by and bag up the bird. Then I'll take a look around. In the meantime, you sit tight and keep your doors locked. I'll get some extra officers to keep an eye on the neighborhood, too."

She nodded gratefully but also experienced the sharp sensation of fear in her stomach.

"Okay, detective. As long as you think it's safe."

By the time her last mumbled words escaped into the air, Brodsky had already disconnected the call.

* * * * *

"I didn't see anything else odd," Brodsky told Anna after almost an hour of walking through the Corvo Hollows property. "Hopefully, the bird will be enough to get us a hit."

"What do you mean?"

"We can dust the bird's feathers for fingerprints."

"Wow, really? That's crazy!"

"Yeah, it's pretty neat technology. They call it a quasar machine. I'm not one of the lab techs, so I'm not completely sure how it works. But if there's anything on those feathers, it might lead us straight to the killer."

"Thank you, Detective," she said with the hopeful tone of their conversation.

"If it works, don't thank me, thank the Scottish researchers who developed the tech. Along with *CSI*, because that's what apparently inspired the idea, believe it or not."

"I'll be thanking all of you," she said. "How long does it take?"

"We should have results in a couple hours," he responded.

CHAPTER TWENTY-FOUR

"What can you tell me about the woman who reported this bird? Anna Collins, right?"

Detective Brodsky paused for an imperceptible beat while trying to gauge the intent behind the newly arrived FBI agent's words. Brodsky had been on edge since returning to the station and discovering that the latest murder has brought the FBI riding into town like the cavalry. Truth be told, no cop worth their salt wanted to share a case with the feds. The stink of failure wafted through the entire station and was accompanied by stiff handshakes and phony smiles.

"Anna's been very helpful," Brodsky said with the most neutral tone he could muster. "Did you get a match on the prints?"

"We did," the tall, thin special agent in an immaculately tailored suit responded. "Follow me. We need to talk."

The two men disappeared into an interrogation room as Jones pondered the meaning behind the agent's words.

* * * * *

A sharp rapping slightly shook Anna's door in the frame. Startled, she jumped up from the couch. Jaxon's eyes instantly transformed from happy to concerned, and he walked to the door behind her. Anna hesitantly unlatched the door's locks and opened it just enough to peer outside. Brodsky's face greeted her, and she exhaled a sigh of relief.

"Hello, Detective," she said warmly.

"Hi, Anna," Brodsky replied. "Can I come in?"

"Of course."

Anna opened the door, and Brodsky almost visibly recoiled as he met Jaxon's gaze.

She has a boyfriend? Brodsky thought in dismay. Even though he knew he couldn't date Anna, the realization that she had another man in her life punched him in the gut. Trying to regain his composure – and his professionalism – Brodsky walked into the apartment.

"I need to talk to you about the, um, incident you reported earlier," Brodsky said, unsure if he should reveal anything else in front of Anna's visitor.

"Thank you for coming back so quickly! Oh, and Detective, this is Jaxon. Jaxon, this is Detective Brodsky."

The two men grunted hello to each other and shook hands. The intensity of Jaxon's handshake made one thing clear: he saw Brodsky's interest in Anna and wanted to stake his claim in an unmistakable way.

"Can we speak in private?" Brodsky inquired.

Before Anna could reply, Jaxon squeezed her hand, kissed her cheek, and said, "I'll leave you two alone. Anna, I'll be in the bedroom if you need me."

She smiled as Jaxon sauntered away.

"Anna," Brodsky began uncomfortably. "Did you happen to touch that bird before I came over earlier?"

Confusion flooded her eyes and she sputtered out, "No. Of course not," with a repulsed shudder.

"Think back carefully. Are you absolutely certain you didn't disturb it in any way? Or did anyone else touch it, like maybe Jaxon?"

"No, not that I know of. Jaxon didn't find out about it until after you left, and I was too grossed out to go anywhere near it. Why do you ask?"

Brodsky shifted from his left to his right foot and then back again, stalling for time and trying to get his own discomfort under control.

"The FBI is working on the murders now. Two of their agents arrived this morning."

"That's great!" she said before taking in his somber expression. "But what does that have to do with the bird?"

"They have access to a fingerprint database that goes way beyond our access codes. It contains millions of criminal and civil fingerprints. We were able to pull prints off the bird feathers and a match was found."

"That sounds like good news...but you don't seem happy about it?"

"Anna...the FBI is going to be here any minute, so I'm just going to spit this out. The prints they found are yours."

Shock twisted her visage and a fresh batch of confusion swam into her eyes.

"How is that possible? I *didn't* touch it."

Brodsky's resolve to take his personal feelings out of the equation melted at her response, despite the scars that were already forming on his heart due to Jaxon's existence.

"I know you didn't," he said softly. "The FBI doesn't know that, though, and they're going to be here any minute."

Sweat broke out on Anna's lower back and forehead. If he didn't trust his intuition so much, Brodsky might have seen this as a sign of guilt. He simply couldn't bring himself to believe she'd been misleading him, no matter what Special Agent Anthony Russo thought.

"Listen carefully, Anna. We don't have much time. When they get here, you have to tell them everything exactly as you've told it to me. They'll try to confuse you, so take your time and answer carefully. Do you understand?"

"Yes, but I didn't do anything wrong?"

Sighing and longing to hug her, Brodsky said, "That doesn't always matter."

As the last syllable left his lips, a harsh knock shook the front door again. Anna nervously opened the door and allowed Special Agent Russo to enter.

"Brodsky," Russo said with a nod in the detective's direction. "Ms. Collins? I'm Special Agent Russo with the Federal Bureau of Investigations. This is my partner, Special Agent Blake."

Brodsky knew his thoughts were biased, but he couldn't help forming an even more negative opinion upon seeing the two FBI agents together. *They look exactly like the type of assholes who would rough up a suspect and laugh about it later.*

"We understand you've provided some information to the local police about the recent spate of murders?" Blake said.

"The bird you found is definitely concerning due to its decapitated state," Russo took over. "What I can't figure out, though, is why it has your fingerprints all over it."

"I don't know," she said with a mixture of confusion and fear. "I *didn't* touch it."

Russo's steel blue eyes narrowed as he fixed her with laser-focused vision. This had long been one of his favorite intimidation techniques. He appeared to casually push his sandy brown hair back with his right hand, although this action was a calculated move meant to make him appear more like an everyday guy. He knew some perps and witnesses found it to be endearing, and he'd always believed in using every possible trick in his arsenal to get to the bottom of each case.

"Are you sure? I mean, if something like that showed up on my front doorstep, my wife would be so terrified that her first instinct might be to try to toss it away. And my son, well, he'd probably want to try to reattach the head," Russo chuckled as his partner cracked an unfriendly smile.

It didn't matter to Russo that both of these comments were lies. Hell, he didn't even have a wife and son. He never let any moral quibbles over telling white lies stand in the way of getting a confession, though.

"I'm sure. I *never* touched it."

"You see, that's a problem for me. Because if you didn't touch it, how did your fingerprints get all over the wings?"

When she didn't immediately provide an answer, Russo decided to push her further.

"Is it possible that you wanted a little more attention from the local police department? Maybe even from a certain handsome detective? Perhaps that made you feel good?"

Her mouth hung agape at the FBI agent's insinuations. Brodsky also clearly took umbrage at Russo's remarks.

"I don't think..." Brodsky began before Russo cut him off.

"Stop. I want to hear from Ms. Collins right now. And *only* Ms. Collins."

The look that passed between the two men was strong and heated enough to create diamonds out of coal.

"I really don't know what to tell you," Anna mumbled. "I didn't touch it, and I certainly didn't kill the bird myself. That's ludicrous!"

"What else am I supposed to think? That your fingerprints walked over to the bird and affixed themselves to its feathers without your knowledge?"

Anna's cheeks turned red from anger.

"Listen, I've had enough of your ridiculous accusations. I don't know what you're trying to do here, but it's *not* true. I *never* touched that bird. Now, why don't you focus on something more important like busting the killers?"

"Killers?" Russo asked.

"Huh?"

"You said killers. Plural. As if you know them."

"I'm pretty damn sure they're my neighbors. Didn't anyone tell you that?"

"Ah, yes. I did hear something about that," Russo admitted. "What do you have against your neighbors, anyway?"

Throughout her life, Anna had remained quiet through far too many negative comments. She'd tried to ignore her sister's blatant racism, no matter how upset it made her. She'd allowed her mother to say awful things without slapping her in response. She'd even let a few bullying comments slip by rather than get into a confrontation. But this line of questioning had finally pushed her too far.

"What do I have against them?" she said with a rapidly increasing volume. "Gee, I don't know. Maybe the fact that they tried to get inside my house a couple of months ago and now it constantly sounds like they're killing people? Is that enough of a reason for you?"

Russo had rattled her, and it made him smile. Whether she had something to do with the murders or was truly an innocent bystander, he always preferred his suspects to be riled up. That was when the truth tended to come out.

"Why are you so angry, Anna?"

"Come on, are you serious?" Brodsky interrupted.

"You're dismissed, Detective," Russo said.

"What?"

"You heard him," Blake sneered. "You're dismissed. We'll finish this interview without you. Go back to the station and wait for us."

Panic took over as Anna watched Brodsky reluctantly leave her apartment. Then it hit her; she wasn't alone with the combative agents. Jaxon was in the next room, and that helped her relax a tiny bit.

"I'm going to ask you one more time. Why are you so angry?" Russo repeated.

"People are getting murdered, and instead of doing something about it, you're here asking me crazy questions about a bird, that's why," she yelled. "I didn't touch that stupid bird. I have no idea how it got my fingerprints on it. Isn't that something you're supposed to be able to figure out, Mr. FBI man?"

Now we're getting somewhere, Russo thought.

"You're absolutely right. That is something I'm supposed to be able to figure out. And I'm going to. I'm pretty sure you just wanted to get some attention. It happens all the time during cases like this. But if it turns out that you're actually...well, let's just say that this would be a good time to start talking. If you wait, everything will get much worse. That's a promise."

"I. Didn't. Do. ANYTHING!"

"Okay, ma'am. We'll see ourselves out then," Russo said with a shark-like grin.

I've got her right where I want her. She'll crack soon, just like all the rest.

CHAPTER TWENTY-FIVE

"Is being an asshole your typical strategy for getting information?" Brodsky gruffly asked Russo.

"Is having the hots for a potential witness or even suspect your typical MO?" Russo replied.

Brodsky tried to avoid letting Russo know just how right he was, but he couldn't stop his cheeks from flooding with warmth. He decided to try a different, less antagonistic tactic with the FBI agent.

"Do you really think she could be the killer?" he asked with all of the former feistiness removed from his tone.

Russo appeared to contemplate the question for a second before responding.

"Probably not. But who knows, right? I'm pretty sure she just wanted your attention, but that's certainly a psychotic way of going about it."

"Yeah, right," Brodsky muttered to himself.

"What's that?" Russo said.

"Why would she be trying to get my attention – or any other man's, for that matter – when she has a boyfriend?"

Russo frowned as he considered this new information. It didn't fit with his preconceived notions, but Anna wouldn't be the first person in the world to continue flirting while in a relationship.

"I bet you twenty bucks she'll call here again with another made-up incident within the next week," Russo offered.

"That's ridiculous."

"Why? Because you're afraid you'll lose?"

Brodsky wasn't usually tempted by such obvious jabs at his masculinity. The disappointment of seeing Anna with another man had left a sour taste in his mouth, though, and he was eager to expunge it somehow. Focusing on a silly little bet – that would almost certainly net him twenty dollars by the end of the week – seemed like a viable distraction.

"You're on," Brodsky said while sticking out his hand.

The two men firmly shook hands to seal the deal.

"I still think we should try to find out how the bird ended up on her doorstep. It could have something to do with her suspicious neighbors we've been watching."

Russo barely stifled his amusement.

"Sure, whatever you say. I tell you what; if you want to follow-up on the bird angle so badly, I'll leave that for you and Jones to handle. Meanwhile, my partner and I will work on the real case."

*You son-of-a...*Brodsky thought. The temptation to punch someone had never been higher, but decking an FBI agent wasn't going to help him continue moving up the chain. Despite being able to control himself, Russo's words made Brodsky so angry that he went outside to have another 'forbidden' cigarette. He hated lying to his girlfriend Susie about them – if they were even still together, after their last argument – and was beginning to hate himself even more for his unprofessional interest in Anna.

* * * * *

"Are you okay?" Jaxon asked.

"Yeah," Anna said in a clipped voice.

Jaxon attempted to put his arms around her, but Anna squirmed away. She didn't want anyone to try to defuse her righteous anger. She couldn't believe that the FBI thought she'd staged the entire thing.

"What a load of crap!" she said. "Did you hear what that incompetent agent said to me?"

"Yes, that's why I wanted to..."

Anna didn't wait for Jaxon to finish. She'd spent much of her life being spoken over or cut off, and she wasn't going to sit back and politely wait for her turn right now.

"The entire thing is ridiculous!"

She headed toward the front door and picked up her keys.

"Hey, where are you going?" Jaxon asked with concern scrunching his eyebrows.

"I'm going to ask Rene if she saw anything."

"Want me to go with you?"

She hesitated for a beat. Her anger wanted to propel her forward alone, but she really enjoyed having Jaxon by her side.

Misreading her hesitation, Jaxon said, "It's okay, I'll go. But call me later if you need to talk, all right?"

She nodded and kissed him quickly on the lips.

"Thanks for understanding," she said as they both exited her apartment.

Relief washed over Anna as Jaxon walked away without any hint of anger. *So, this is what it's like to date someone who actually acts their age,* she mused. She could definitely get used to this.

By the time Anna had walked to the other side of the building, her anger had started to dissipate. Her first few harsh, ground-shaking footsteps had turned into the slightly hard walk of a person on a mission. Relief swirled around her for the second time in as many minutes when she noticed Rene's interior lights shining brightly. Before she could even knock, Rene had the door open.

"Anna!" she exclaimed with her characteristic enthusiasm. "Come in, come in. How are you? How are things with Jaxon?"

"They're great, but that's not why I'm here."

"Oh?" Rene said with a dampened tone as she took in Anna's expression. "What happened?"

"Did you happen to see anything weird today?"

"Like what?" Rene laughed. "I see weird stuff around here every day. You're going to need to be more specific, hon."

Rene's jovial manner had once left Anna a bit nervous, but now, she'd warmed to it. So much so, in fact, that hearing Rene make one of her little jokes soothed her frayed nerves.

"I found a dead bird outside my door earlier today."

"Aww. That poor bird." Rene's eyes teared up. "But what does that have to do with neighborhood weirdness?"

"You might want to brace yourself for this," Anna said reflexively in response to Rene's unexpected emotional display. "The bird wasn't just dead, Rene. Its head had been cut off."

"Oh my god. Who would *do* something so twisted?"

"That's exactly what I want to know. I called the cops about it, but they were less than helpful."

"Of course," Rene said as her head bobbed up and down. "Can't trust them to take care of anything, can we?"

Anna hadn't known about Rene's apparent contempt for the police, which she thought was a bit weird considering what Rene's husband did for a living. Nevertheless, she continued her tale.

"It's the oddest thing, though. I never touched that bird..."

"Eww! Of course not," Rene agreed.

"But they claim my fingerprints were on its feathers."

Rene studied her neighbor for a second as intrigue and sympathy fought for dominance on her face.

"They must have botched the entire thing," Rene responded with a snort of derision. "Tell me, did they pull prints from anything else?"

"Come to think of it, I'm pretty sure they took prints from my screen door during one of their visits."

"That's it, then! Mystery solved. They clearly screwed up and ran the wrong prints."

Anna considered this possibility and liked the idea, even if she wasn't entirely convinced it was the truth.

"The FBI agents were so rude to me about it, too."

"FBI agents?" Rene asked with renewed interest. "Were they at least good looking?"

"If you like the querulous type, then sure. They annoyed the crap out of me and kept insisting I planted the dead bird there myself to capture the attention of Detective Brodsky."

"Now *that* sounds like a worthy endeavor."

Anna shook her head at Rene's constant need to objectify every man within a two-mile radius.

"Maybe, but that's *not* what happened. Besides, I have a boyfriend now. Why in the world would I do something so macabre to get the attention of a cop I'm not interested in?"

"You wouldn't. I might do something like that – minus the bird decapitation, naturally – but that's just not your style. So, let me guess. You think the new neighbors did it, am I right?"

"I can't imagine who else it could have been," Anna replied.

"Maybe you are on to something. Or," Rene said with more gentleness than usual, "maybe you really need to start getting some more sleep. Jaxon told me what happened the other day with the knocking sound. He said he didn't hear anything, hon."

Dammit, Jaxon, Anna thought.

"Wait, when did Jaxon talk to you?"

"We ran into each other in the parking lot. Don't tell me you're mad?"

Anna's hesitation said it all.

"He didn't mean any harm by it, Anna. I could tell he was just really worried about you. And so am I. That guy's a catch and a half, so try not to read him the riot act *too* much. You don't want to let someone like that slip through your fingers."

"You're right," Anna said to bring the topic to a close. She also made a mental note to talk to Jaxon about protecting her privacy.

CHAPTER TWENTY-SIX

It had been three days since Russo's bullying attempt at getting information out of Anna. The FBI agent couldn't help but make a connection between that and the fact that no new bodies had been discovered. As he looked through the case files and reflected on her visible anger, he began to wonder if maybe, just maybe, there was more to her than met the eye.

She doesn't look like a killer, he thought. *But neither did Marie Noe, and she killed eight of her own babies.*

He picked up a tiny stress ball off his temporary desk inside the local police station and squeezed it again and again. He didn't actually use it to relieve stress. Instead, the rhythmic motion of squeezing it, rotating it across his palm, and then squeezing it again helped him get out of his head just enough that inspiration sometimes struck.

Russo's team back at the Detroit FBI Field Office had already run Anna's information through every possible criminal database and had come up empty. They also knew that her prints were on file in the civil database because she'd done an art internship at a local school several years ago. But what if there was something in her civil or medical records that could point him in the right direction? With no other good leads, he picked up the phone and asked the first agent on the other end of the line to conduct a different type of search.

* * * * *

Anna's anger at the FBI agent had felt good at the time, but she'd been suffering for it ever since. Unfortunately, having any big outbursts of emotion or energy could derail her physical health for days by bringing on a very painful fibromyalgia flare.

She probably wouldn't have stopped herself from getting so animated even if she'd known for sure what the outcome would be, though. After all, if she didn't stand up for herself, who else was going to do it? This idea had been put aside to her detriment far too many times already, and the last thing she wanted to do was give the FBI a reason to suspect her for a crime she didn't commit.

Her relationship with Jaxon had suffered a bit of a setback after Rene told her they'd discussed the knocking sound – or lack thereof, according to him. Despite Rene's protestations to the contrary and Anna's initial urge to forgive and forget, the ease with which Jaxon had violated her privacy left her uncertain if she should trust him.

Someone else had spilled her secrets a few years ago, and it hadn't ended well. That privacy breach had left her suspicious of other people's intentions. Her sister and therapist kept trying to get her to move forward and let it go, and she thought that Jaxon – along with her growing friendship with Rene – had been a step in the right direction. Now, though? The entire thing left her with a bad taste in her mouth and an unsettled stomach.

Her thoughts were interrupted when an alert went off on her smartphone. *Thunderstorms will begin in 18 minutes. Some may be severe*, it said. "18 minutes, huh? Not 15, not 20, but exactly 18," she laughed as Poe lifted her gray head in response to Anna's words. Anna noted the almost overflowing trash can in the kitchen and decided she'd better wrap it up and take it to the dumpster before the skies opened up with yet another summer thunderstorm.

Electricity seemed to course through the air as she hefted the stinky trash bag outside. *I've got to stop putting broccoli bits in the trash.*

A bolt of lightning ripped across the distant sky, but the accompanying thunder was just out of her auditory reach. The sight of it, combined with the distinctive smell in the air, made it clear a strong storm would soon unleash itself in the Hollows.

A neighborhood stray wagged its tail excitedly near the dumpster. She couldn't see what treat he had chosen for his meal yet, but the medium-sized, brown and white mutt appeared to be even happier than usual. Anna had encountered this dog numerous times, and its pleasant disposition never seemed to waver, even though it didn't have a permanent home.

"Hi Chuck," she called to him while crossing the remaining distance between them. She had no idea what his name was – if he even had one – but she'd taken to calling him Chuck after running into him for the third time last summer.

Usually, Chuck would lift his muzzle from his food long enough to greet her with his distinctive grin, but this time he kept chomping down on something.

Must be really good. Maybe someone left some meat for him. Corvo Hollows management had sent out several notices asking people not to feed the stray animals, but no one listened. They'd been accepted as part of the community instead, and it had become common to see Chuck and a couple of stray cats dining by one of the dumpsters.

Anna walked around Chuck, tossed her bag in the dumpster, and then decided to take a peek at what had him so enraptured. She petted his back and said, "Whatcha' got there, Chuck?" since his body blocked her view.

Chuck turned around and attempted to lick her hand, like usual. Crimson red rivulets of blood dripped from his mouth onto his chest and she jumped back in terror.

The dog cocked its head to the side for a second as if inquiring why she'd reacted so differently than usual. She didn't see any malice in his eyes, nor were there any immediately obvious signs of rabies. If it hadn't been for his bloody face and chest, Chuck would have looked as happy and benign as usual.

Torn between her desire to run screaming from the animal and to see what in the world he'd been eating, she steeled herself and slowly went back to Chuck's side. His tail wagging picked up in response, and he turned back to his food. Before she had a chance to creep around him, Chuck proudly picked up his prize and turned around to show it to her.

The remnants of a human hand dropped from his mouth, and he nosed it toward her as if to say, "Here, human. Have some. It's delicious!"

Her scream erupted into the air in tandem with the rumbling of quickly approaching thunder. Confused, Chuck bolted for the nearby woods as Anna ran back to her apartment.

CHAPTER TWENTY-SEVEN

"Anna, hold on. I can't understand you. Take a deep breath and tell me again, okay?"

Detective Brodsky's words did nothing to soothe the rapidity of her heart, but she did do as he asked. Two deep breaths later, she tried again to tell him what she'd just seen.

"Chuck was eating a...a...it's so awful! You need to come out here, Detective!"

"Who is Chuck?"

"The dog!"

"Okay, and what was he eating?"

"A hand!"

He still wasn't one-hundred percent sure what she was saying, but with everything else that had happened, Brodsky knew he needed to check on her right away.

"Hang tight. I'll be there in ten minutes."

As he grabbed his rain jacket, he called to his partner.

"Jones! We've got to roll!"

* * * * *

Twenty minutes later, Brodsky, Jones, and Anna stood in the rain looking inside the dumpster enclosure. Anna had calmed down enough by the time they'd arrived to tell them her story, and they'd immediately headed out to look for the evidence.

"Is this what you saw, ma'am?" Jones asked as he pointed toward a disembodied hand.

"Yes!" she immediately said before taking a closer look at the item in question. "I mean, no. That's *not* it. What is that, anyway? Some type of prop?"

Brodsky and Jones looked at each other uncomfortably as the truth became clear. The hand was nothing more than part of an old mannequin. It did have a couple of bite marks on it, too, which seemed to indicate it was exactly what she'd seen the dog chewing on.

After a few more minutes of poking around, they spotted the rest of the mannequin inside the dumpster beneath a mountain of trash bags. "Looks like there's nothing here, boss," Jones said quietly.

"Okay, wait a minute. I *know* how this looks, but I *swear* there was a real hand. Two of the fingers were already gone, and Chuck had blood all over his face. It was also on the ground. There's got to still be some there. Please, look again."

Brodsky sighed internally. He knew he'd just lost twenty dollars to Russo. Still, to put Anna's mind at ease, he looked around the area one more time with his flashlight, searching for any hint of blood.

"I don't see anything, Anna. I'm sorry," Brodsky said.

"But it *was* there. Maybe the rain...?"

"Yeah, it's possible it could have been washed away. But there's really nothing else I can do at this time. Let's get you back inside so you can dry off, okay?"

The detectives walked her back to her front door. Frustration and shame lit her cheeks as red as Rudolph's nose. She had been so certain she'd seen a real human hand...but what if she was wrong?

"Call me if you see anything else out of the ordinary," Brodsky said a few minutes later. His words were reassuring, but their tone was not. She knew her credibility had just taken a huge hit that it might never recover from.

After the detectives left, she locked the door, slid to the floor, and her face fell into her hands. *Am I going crazy?*

* * * * *

"You got something to tell me, Brodsky?" Russo said with a shit-eating grin. His partner, Special Agent Joshua Blake, couldn't suppress a mean-spirited laugh.

Brodsky frowned at how quickly the agents had found out. "Yeah, yeah," the detective said. "Here you go." He handed Russo a bent, slightly tattered twenty-dollar bill and turned to leave.

"Hold on, there. Bets and jokes aside, I need to talk to you about something."

Brodsky tried to remove the look of disdain from his face as he turned back around and followed Russo into the office he and Jones usually shared.

"I've got something interesting to show you," Russo said with a hint of smugness that set Brodsky's pride on fire. "Have a seat."

That's it, asshole. Rub it in, Brodsky thought.

A thin file folder flopped on the desk in front of the detective. Out of habit, he instantly picked it up before asking, "what's this?"

"Why don't you look through it, first? And then *you* can tell me what you think it means."

Certain that the folder's contents were some type of trick but unable to stop his curiosity, Brodsky opened it and glanced at the first page. He read only a few words before looking up. Puzzled, he said, "you ran a full civil and medical background check on Anna Collins? Even though you were convinced she was just looking for attention? Why?"

"Because the criminal check came back clean, and I needed to dot all my i's and cross all my t's. I suggest you read through it."

Brodsky's eyes returned to the thin stack of papers and his puzzlement quickly changed to dismay. A few minutes later, he sat the folder back on the desk and hoped that Russo hadn't noticed the slight trembling in his right hand.

"Well?" Russo asked.

"She's been in a psych ward before?" Brodsky asked, hoping against hope that Russo would tell him the entire thing had been a sick practical joke.

"Yup."

"Wait, how did you even get this information without a warrant?"

"I'm FBI, Brodsky. Most people will say or do almost anything to get us to go away. Everyone has a guilty conscience about something, you know."

"That's not legal..." Brodsky protested.

"It's legal enough," Russo fired back. "Besides, you should be grateful. I just saved you a lot of trouble. It looks like your little crush is an entire popcorn bucket full of crazy. Now you can stop being at her beck and call and start working on the real case."

Brodsky's thoughts whirred like an overheated laptop computer. Not only did Russo break several protocols to obtain this information – most likely for no good reason other than lording it over him – but the agent's take on mental health issues left a lot to be desired.

Brodsky's anger flared through his body, but he knew better than to express it. He stood up, hoping to make a quick escape, when Russo said, "if you're going, take that folder with you. Be sure to flip through it again if you get any other misguided notions about Mrs. Coocoo."

Russo laughed as if he'd made the wittiest joke of all time. Brodsky, meanwhile, barely managed to leave the office without taking out his anger on the agent's face.

* * * * *

Anna had fallen asleep after sobbing about the day's bad experiences. Her self-confidence had been rattled to its core. When she awoke several hours later, the world seemed a lot duller and flatter.

"Did any of it really happen?" she asked the air.

More than three years had passed since her struggle with mental illness. Since that time, Anna had made a lot of progress at repairing her ability to believe in herself and her own perceptions of the world around her. She'd also been off her anti-depressants for about a year now.

She thought about texting her therapist, but the fear of where that could lead quickly stopped her. The last time, she *had* really needed some help, but not the type she'd received. Her fiancé at that time, Scott, had taken her late-night admission about depression and occasional suicidal thoughts way too far, and it landed her in the hospital for two weeks.

As if everyone doesn't think dark thoughts from time-to-time, she'd rationalized then, and she still believed that sentiment three years later. What had changed in the interim was that her dark thoughts were far less frequent now, and they almost never veered too far into the pitch-black areas of her psyche.

With these ruminations swirling in her head, she failed to notice the light tapping that seemed to emanate from the upper edge of her apartment's shared back wall. Tux was spooked by it, though, and he ran from the room.

"What's wrong, kitty?" she called after him.

A loud thump shattered the silence of her apartment, following by several knocking noises.

Not again, she internally pleaded, uncertain what to do. As the sounds continued, her gaze fell on her phone. *I could record it!* Excited by her new idea, she jumped up, thumbed open the voice memo app, and pressed record while moving as close to the source of the sound as possible.

This will prove I'm not crazy! Her future vindication almost made her dance for joy. Then an insidious, doubtful voice in the back of her head broke through her singular moment of happiness. *Or it will prove that I'm nuttier than a fruitcake.*

CHAPTER TWENTY-EIGHT

Brodsky's phone rang. His hand fumbled in the dark and he almost said, "sorry, babe" out of habit before remembering that he and Susie had finally broken up after yet another shouting match. He didn't know how she did it, but Susie always managed to light a fire inside of him that couldn't be contained at a normal volume.

Of course, Susie started most of their fights. For a little while, he'd contemplated the possibility that she enjoyed the drama and went out of her way to manufacture it. Their breakup earlier this evening seemed to prove otherwise.

"Hello?" he said in the slurred, sleepy haze of someone who had just woken up after a really bad night.

"Brodsky, it's Russo. We've got another body. Pick up Jones and get your ass over here. I'll text you the address."

Before Brodsky could even think about forming a response, the line went dead. He rubbed sleep from his eyes and wearily dragged his body back into the same, slightly crumpled suit he'd worn during his normal shift of the day. There was no way around it; tonight was going to be another shitshow.

* * * * *

Morning had woken Anna from a fitful sleep. Her first action was to press play on her smartphone, followed by three more subsequent playthroughs. She sat enraptured and terrified by everything her phone had captured. It wasn't a delusion, nor did she dream the sounds from last night. She had indisputable proof now. The knocking was real.

Tears of relief streamed down her cheeks and splashed onto her shirt. After a fifth playthrough, she finally sat her phone down and issued a harsh fit of laughter into the silence that enveloped her apartment. The knocking had stopped hours ago, just as quickly as it had begun. More importantly, she could now give something much more concrete than suspicions and disappearing limbs to Detective Brodsky.

If he'll ever take my call again.

A text message from Rene caught her attention.

"Hi neighbor! Want to grab some breakfast? My treat!"

Anna held the phone between her hands for a moment while trying to decide what to do. Her joints ached, like usual, and she had a slight headache from not sleeping enough. She also wanted to get this evidence into Brodsky's hands ASAP. However, the idea of a nice breakfast intrigued her, as did the opportunity to tell someone else about the sounds she'd recorded.

"Sounds good! Meet in 20 minutes?" Anna replied.

"Perfect!"

* * * * *

Brodsky's bleary eyes tried to focus on Russo. The two had worked the crime scene with Blake, Jones, and several other officers since four a.m., and it was now a little after eight in the morning.

On any other day, he'd be headed to the station now after getting a good night's sleep. But thanks to his fight with Susie, followed by the early morning crime call, he was operating on about three hours of sleep and more cups of coffee than he could count.

Russo's fingers tapped on the desk one after another in a repeating pattern. Brodsky didn't like the room's ambiance; it seemed stuffy and full of negative energy.

"Okay, I'm just going to spit this out, Brodsky."

Despite making such a declarative sentence, Russo paused momentarily, as if he still needed to get his words, or his nerves, together. Every passing second sucked more air out of the room. Brodsky had the sensation of being led to the gallows for a crime he hadn't committed.

"Anna Collins called you yesterday about a so-called decapitated human hand. Then lo and behold, a new body shows up, and it's missing a hand. Do you see where I'm going with this?"

"Honestly?" Brodsky replied. "No, I really don't. The hand in question was from a mannequin. That's been well established. What could you possibly think these two things have to do with each other?"

"Have you not read the coroner's report, Brodsky? That's pretty sloppy on your part, I'd say," Russo said with icy contempt. "Here, let me catch you up to speed. Our male vic was murdered earlier in the day at a different location and then moved. The time of death would have been at least a couple hours before Anna called you."

Russo stopped and stared at Brodsky for a few seconds, waiting for the puzzle pieces to connect. When Brodsky still offered him nothing, he sighed with exasperation and slammed his palm against the desk.

"Wake up, man! She's been playing you this whole time. She's either the killer, or she knows the killer. How else could she have gotten that detail right?"

"Wait a minute, back up," Brodsky said. "You're trying to tell me that you think she's the killer, and yet she called in an incident with a disembodied hand to accomplish what, exactly?"

"Guilty conscience got the better of her? Perhaps she wants to get caught and is feeding you clues?"

"Or maybe, just maybe, her neighbors actually are offing people and she *did* find some real evidence by the dumpster. And

maybe the neighbors realized that and took steps to cover their tracks before we arrived."

Russo let out a long, low whistle. "Wow, you must have it bad to concoct such a twisted narrative to fit your view of her. I've got news for you, Detective. It's time to stop trying to screw her and do you damn job!"

Resisting the immediate temptation to toss steaming hot coffee in Russo's face, Brodsky responded through clenched teeth. "Let's see what the unis have to say."

"What unis?"

"The team I assigned to watch and trail her neighbors," Brodsky said incredulously.

"I called them off that job two days ago. What a waste of resources," Russo spat.

"You did what?" Brodsky's anger echoed throughout the entire police station. "Why would you do that, and without even telling me first?"

"Because you're not in charge anymore. This is my case, and I'll decide how our resources are best allocated. Now, I suggest you adjust your attitude, Detective," Russo responded, turning each syllable in 'detective' into a verbal bullet. "If you dare question my judgment again, you'll be writing traffic tickets again so fast your head will spin."

* * * * *

Clinking silverware filled the moderately-sized restaurant with the best breakfast in town. Anna and Rene had caught each other up on the little details of their lives. Rene had expressed unhappiness over Anna's decision to not immediately forgive and forget what she viewed as Jaxon's minor faux pas. Anna had sat properly enthralled as Rene described her latest Skype chat with her deployed husband.

"I have something I want you to listen to," Anna said as the sounds of her heartbeat filled her head. Anxious to be believed, and afraid of somehow still looking like a fool, she pulled up the recording on her phone and pressed play.

At first, nothing but static came through the phone's tiny speaker. Within seconds, though, the distinct but distant sound of knocking filled the space between them.

Rene's face scrunched up in confusion as Anna said, "See? There it is."

"There's what, hon?"

"The knocking sound. From the neighbors' apartment? I recorded this last night when they were at it again."

"Maybe it's too noisy in here for me to hear it," Rene said carefully. "I know, I'll use my earbuds." Rene dug through her bag for a moment, saying "they're in here somewhere, I know it," followed an agonizing thirty seconds later – which felt like thirty minutes to Anna – with a triumphant "ah-ha! Here they are."

Rene listened closely to the recording once, then turned the volume all the way up before hitting play again. Concern filled her eyes as she removed the earbuds and laid the phone down on the table. She reached across the table and took Anna's hand.

"I'm sorry, hon...but I couldn't hear anything. Maybe I listened to the wrong recording?"

"That's impossible," Anna said. She quickly scrolled through her phone to confirm what she already knew; Rene had heard the right recording three times now. How could she claim she didn't hear the knocking noise?

Her panic-stricken eyes met Rene's. Anna could see a volume of unspoken words sitting behind her friend's eyes. The most prominent appeared to be concern, but pity had joined the party, too, along with a hint of disbelief. Anna's fears of the previous evening crashed back down on her aching shoulders, and she had to flee to the restroom to avoid becoming the ultimate cliché by crying in public.

CHAPTER TWENTY-NINE

The rain returned with a vengeance that afternoon, and Anna sequestered herself from the world. She'd barely spoken two words to Rene on their way home from the restaurant, and she'd since ignored multiple texts and calls from Rene and Jaxon.

She tried to distract herself by working on a new book cover, but her mind kept wandering so much that she needed to click undo dozens of times to erase her numerous mistakes. She finally gave up on the idea of producing quality work and took out her negative energy on the treadmill instead, much to the dismay of her aching muscles and joints.

After, she calmed herself with a lukewarm shower and snuggled under the blankets. Anna prepared herself for an evening filled with critical thoughts, but her body mercifully shut down for once at the exact right time.

* * * * *

More than twelve hours later, Anna awoke to find the sun shining brightly through her bedroom window. Initially confused about the time of day, she quickly realized she'd actually slept for half a day.

If nothing else, finding out I'm going crazy was a good way to get some sleep for once.

Anna was torn between going to her therapy appointment in a couple of hours and reaching out to Jaxon in an attempt to make up. On the one hand, she could probably use a therapy visit, considering what she'd learned yesterday during breakfast. Yet she was concerned that opening up about it would lead to nothing but bad things.

Meanwhile, a heavy weight sat in her stomach when she thought about her harsh reaction to Jaxon expressing his concerns to Rene. Now that both of them had confirmed the noises weren't real, Anna couldn't stand the idea of continuing to punish Jaxon for her mistake.

Unsure who she was going to select from her phone book until the very last minute, she went into her texts and fired off a quick message to Jeani.

"Sorry to do this at the last minute, but I'm having a very bad flare this morning. Can we reschedule? Thanks."

Guilt besieged her as the floating text bubbles verified Jeani was already responding.

"No worries, Anna. Get some rest and feel better. Same time next week?"

Anna confirmed her next appointment before spending an inordinate amount of time crafting the perfect text to Jaxon. In the end, she wasn't pleased with it, but clicked 'send' anyway.

"Hey you. Sorry about the last few days. I know you were just trying to help. Forgive me? I'd love to see you tonight."

Before her already frazzled nerves could make the situation even worse, Jaxon texted back.

"No forgiveness needed. I'm sorry for not considering your privacy. How about I bring over dinner? 6ish?"

Immensely relieved by Jaxon's easy acceptance of her apology, Anna happily returned to a semi-state of normality. She pulled up the latest cover on her MacBook Pro and found it easy to work again. Her digital pencil flowed across the surface of the screen, and she manipulated the results by filling in the empty spaces with a variety of colors and shading techniques.

By lunchtime, she'd completed her latest project and sent it over to the publisher for approval. Suddenly aware that her stomach had been rumbling for a while, she checked out the meager contents of her refrigerator and pantry. It was well past time to go shopping. Rather than focus on that right now, she decided to walk down to the sub shop just outside the community.

A moving truck in the parking lot caught her eye.

I hope it's those weirdos moving out.

A blink of an eye later, the weirdos in question sauntered into the parking lot. Anna's initial instinct was to hide somehow, but there was nothing between her and them, aside from about ten feet of concrete. The man's eyes skipped over her as if he'd never seen her before. The woman, who had dyed her hair light brown and changed her fashion sense yet again squinted her eyes and peered at Anna curiously.

Unwilling to have another encounter with them – and shaken to the core by the thought that they could be committing so many murders that they no longer recognized one of their earlier intended targets – Anna's pace quickened and she soon left them behind.

The sub shop's mixture of delicious and repugnant odors made her happy that her veggie sub was ready and waiting. Ever since developing fibromyalgia, Anna had dealt with sensory issues, particularly in relation to food smells. Therefore, some of her old favorites were now off her personal menu.

Sweat dripped from every pore during the walk back. It was barely noon, and the intensity of the day's heat had already made being outside like sitting inside a sauna. Heat on its own was bad enough, but here in Metro Detroit, she also had to face stiflingly high levels of humidity that turned the air into a swamp.

Today's humidity and heat had combined to produce such a hot, swamp-like environment that she half-expected to see an alligator climb out of the Corvo Hollows neighborhood pond.

Fortunately for the many waterfowl that called the pond home, the closest wild gators were more than eight-hundred miles away.

By the time she got home, she could have sworn the soles of her tennis shoes were melted. With lunch, the heat, and Jaxon occupying her thoughts, she almost walked into an average-sized, dark-skinned woman carrying a kitchen chair.

"Oops, sorry about that!" Anna said.

The woman smiled pleasantly and said, "no worries!"

"I'm Dina," the woman called to Anna as she opened the front door of the unit next door. "Looks like we're neighbors!"

"Hi Dina, I'm Anna. Glad to see someone finally moving into that apartment."

Lying for the second time today? Way to go, Anna, she chided herself. The truth was that she'd relished living next to a vacant unit. The lack of sound had been wonderful, and she'd secretly hoped no one would ever move in again.

The two women exchanged a couple more niceties before entering their respective apartments. Anna spent the next two hours wincing internally each time a loud noise emanated from Dina's side of their shared side wall.

* * * * *

"It's so good to see you," Jaxon whispered in Anna's left ear.

"Mmmm," Anna uttered with pleasure.

The two had been cuddling on the couch since dinner, but now it seemed time to let a bigger spark build between them. He slid back on the couch, pulling her frame against his. Their passions flamed higher with a make-out session that resembled those of Anna's teenage years. But unlike that time period of her life, there was no longer a need to make Jaxon stop for propriety's sake. Instead, she lightly bit the side of his neck to make it clear she wanted to continue.

Jaxon removed her clothing with such efficiency that she almost didn't even notice. He also flipped her onto her back before climbing on top of her. Her body called to his, and he eagerly accepted the charges.

The first thrust made Anna bite her lip and tilt her head back in ecstasy. "Oh my god," she said under her breath. Encouraged by her response, Jaxon slowly picked up the pace until the couch began bucking beneath them. Just as an orgasm threatened to rip her body in half, Anna heard a pounding in the background.

Ignore it, ignore it, ignore it.

Her body retreated from the precipice of pleasure, and Jaxon pushed on, undeterred. As the wall reverberated again, she convinced herself it was nothing more than the new neighbor hanging up some photographs. Holding onto this thought, she managed to tune out the potential evidence of her looming insanity long enough to climax.

They laid silently for a while. Jaxon broke the silence first.

"That was fantastic."

"Yeah..." she responded dreamily.

"But it seemed like you got distracted there for a minute? What happened?"

"I...oh, never mind. It was nothing."

He smiled and kissed her.

CHAPTER THIRTY

In the scant light of the moon, a body moved toward the community dumpster closest to Anna's. The person in question didn't want to be seen, which is exactly why he'd waited until nightfall. He removed a small spray bottle from his pocket, crouched down, and sprayed a substance over the white concrete pad.

He held another item in his hand. Just as the odd light came to life, Rene surprised him by walking around the corner.

"Oh! Wow, you scared me half to death, officer."

"It's detective," Brodsky corrected her out of habit as he rose to his normal standing position.

"Are you happy to see me, or is that a blacklight in your hand?" she tittered.

He eyed her wearily.

"OOOHHH! Let me guess! You're on some type of stakeout, right? Well, I have to say anyone you're searching for is in luck because you look *damn* fine in those pants."

"Um, thanks," Brodsky said. "I'm just following up on something. It's nothing for you to be concerned about, though."

She tossed her trash bag into the dumpster, winked, and said, "whatever you say, officer." The temptation to correct her again fell away when he saw the provocative manner in which she was walking away.

Shaking his head, he used the spray bottle again. Uninterrupted this time, he turned on the black light and shined it against the concrete. Even though it had rained a few times since his last visit to this particular dumpster, he knew that luminol had a good chance of still picking up any traces of blood. A tiny trail glowed brightly under the light. If anything, this revelation created more questions than it answered.

If the dog really was chewing on a human hand, how did it get here? Where did it go? And how did a mannequin hand replace it?

With these unsettling questions plaguing him, Brodsky had to allow the worst one yet to come forward: *is Anna the killer?*

* * * * *

The rain returned with great fervor shortly after Brodsky climbed into his car. It seemed to Anna like the clouds had somehow picked up one of the Great Lakes and were now dropping all of it on top of Metro Detroit.

This theory didn't seem that far off base for anyone unlucky enough to be caught driving that night. Flashfloods quickly appeared in numerous areas, and one of Detroit's main freeways had to shut down due to extensive flooding.

Anna managed to nod off again for the second night in a row. She wished that Jaxon had been able to share her bed, but he'd taken off earlier so he'd be prepared for a big early morning meeting.

Anna stumbled into the bathroom around seven a.m. The linoleum squished under her feet. Moisture seeped between her toes and crept up to the bottom of her ankles.

What the hell?

She fumbled with the light switch and instantly recoiled from the garish glow that flooded the tiny room. Once her eyes were able to focus, she saw a tiny sea of red water standing on the floor.

Oh my god. Is that...blood?

She jumped back out of the bathroom and landed on the slightly soggy carpet. Her eyes squeezed shut in disbelief. When they reopened, she saw the truth; the reddish hue within the linoleum had combined with the soft glow of the room's light to create a subtle red coloring to the standing pool of water. Her imagination had merely taken her eyes' visual cues and turned them into something sinister.

Her head tilted to the ceiling and she groaned. More than half of the ceiling had the swollen appearance of a pregnant woman who is three weeks past her due date. Only a small area had perforated so far. If the rest of the ceiling gave in, her entire apartment would become flooded.

One quick call to the emergency maintenance line later, Anna hastily pulled on some clothes and waited for John, the maintenance tech, to arrive.

* * * * *

"I need to tell you something," Brodsky said as he drove down Ford Road.

"What's up, boss?" Jones asked.

"I went to Corvo Hollows last night...I just couldn't get Russo's damn smirk out of my head, and...well...I guess I wanted to see if I could prove him wrong because I really don't believe his theory about Anna."

Keeping his thoughts to himself, Jones opted to simply nod along, despite the anxious lump forming in his throat.

"I sprayed some luminol on the ground by the dumpster, and it glowed like a Christmas tree. There's definitely been some blood spilled in that area."

Jones chose his words and tone very carefully. "It could be a coincidence, though, right?"

"Sure...but my gut tells me it's not."

The younger detective knew his partner's intuition was rarely wrong, but he grappled a bit with the possibility that Brodsky's feelings for Anna were getting in the way. Finally, he said, "What's our next move, then?"

"I'm still trying to figure that out. For now, let's just try to keep an eye on the Hollows, okay? Russo pulled our uni detail."

Jones agreed while ruminating over how dead Russo was going to be if the cocky FBI agent's decision ended up costing Anna her life.

* * * * *

"Oh, bloody hell," John said to himself. His flashlight showed an entire wading pool sitting in Anna's attic, which had clearly been caused by a new hole in the roof.

He'd been telling the Regional Manager for months that the roof was moments away from busting open, but he'd been ignored. Like usual. The corporate office would have to listen now, but it was going to cost them three times as much as it would have to just fix the damn roof.

"There goes my raise," he muttered.

Even worse, he was now going to be tasked with climbing up on the roof to look for any other holes or obvious weaknesses. The flow of the water trapped in the attic made it clear that at least one more apartment had been affected, so he'd also have to get in there to assess the damage.

John voice-dialed the front office from his Bluetooth as he climbed carefully down the rickety ladder. As expected, the Property Manager met the bad news with his typical attitude, which amounted to a combination of "I really don't care" and "what do you expect me to do about it?"

John issued his daily plea to the universe: please get me out of here or bring me a manager who will actually do their job. Knowing that the Property Manager wouldn't be in a hurry to call the appropriate contractors or to inform the Regional Manager about the damage, John promised Anna he'd be back soon and stepped outside to make a few more calls.

CHAPTER THIRTY-ONE

John had informed Anna that staying in the apartment might be tricky for the next few days. She promptly called her renter's insurance provider and got an approval to temporarily relocate to a hotel down the block. With her cats and most important art equipment packed up, she bid her home adieu.

I hope I don't have to stay gone for too long.

Meanwhile, John and the first contractor struggled to get a shop vac up into the attic. Stan, a water remediation expert, took one look at the mess and whistled a long, low tone.

"That's not going to be an easy fix," Stan grunted as the two finally achieved their initial goal. With everything in place, including a perilously run power line, Stan started the long process of drying the attic. He usually hated spending time in flooded crawlspaces but found himself wishing for something so simple today. At least then a sump pump would have been a viable option.

"Hey, John!" Stan shouted to the man working in the bathroom below.

"Huh?"

"Get over here, will ya?"

John's head poked through the ladder entryway.

"What do you need?"

Stan pointed a flashlight at the attic's back wall. "Do you see how wet that is and how the water keeps trying to flow that way?"

"Yeah, I figured there's another flood in that attic."

"You figured right, my friend. And we really need to get another shop vac in there so that I'm not just fighting against it over here. I'll get one of my guys to come out."

John knew corporate was going to freak out over the cost of two emergency repair contractors, but what else could he do? Rationalizing it as a way to save money in the long-run, he agreed to Stan's suggestion.

I'd better go inform the tenants, John thought as he headed out of Anna's unit.

* * * * *

Forty-five minutes later, John led the newly arrived contractor, Edwin, through the apartment behind Anna's. The tenants weren't home, which was a relief and troublesome at the same time. John always preferred working in an empty apartment, but people could be downright nasty about it when an emergency forced him to enter without giving proper notice.

Edwin climbed up the ladder to check out the damage. "I hate these ladders," he said with a laugh. "They're always so damn rickety!"

"I hear that," John agreed.

An eerie hush fell over the unit as Edwin's laughter died on his lips. Five seconds passed, then ten. Unable to stand the suspense, John said, "Hey, is everything okay up there?"

A pin seemed to pop Edwin's inability to speak or move. He screamed and flew down the ladder. John reached for his arm as the contractor tried to bolt from the apartment.

"What is it, man?"

"I'm not staying here for another second," Edwin said fearfully as he made the sign of the cross and broke free of John's grasp. Confused, John followed him outside in search of answers.

"What's going on?"

Edwin blinked at him and slowed his frantic walk down the sidewalk. "You mean you didn't check it out first?"

"No, I was in the other attic with Stan."

Edwin's countenance was etched with terror and disdain. "You should call the police, and then a priest."

"And tell them what?"

"Tell them the devil has come to town."

CHAPTER THIRTY-TWO

The strobe effect created by multiple camera flashes going off at once made the attic look even more horrifying than Jones had expected. Since partnering up with Brodsky, he'd seen some gnarly things that kept him awake at night and made him push his dinner away. But nothing had ever come close to this.

"I want this entire place photographed within the next ten minutes, people," Russo commanded. "Then it's time to bag it and tag it. We have no idea when our suspects will be home, and I'd like to avoid a lab tech slaughter, all right?"

Jane shivered at the implication as she collected forensics evidence. Sadly, Russo's gruffness wasn't exactly bullshit. She and the other various lab techs, along with the crime scene photographers, weren't exactly well-versed in how to handle themselves around desperate criminals. They usually wouldn't even be here yet, but the evidence in this particular display of viciousness was becoming increasingly compromised by the minute.

Jane glanced around and let the visual imagery truly enter her brain. The attic floor was still flooded, and a few of her co-workers were combing through the standing water in the hopes of finding additional evidence. That left her standing face-to-face with the most gruesome collection of souvenirs she'd ever encountered.

Several disembodied heads leered at her from behind glass. Shelving units had been installed on the attic walls, and each one looked like it belonged in Dr. Frankenstein's laboratory. She grimly noted that there might be enough spare body parts to make an entirely new person.

Brodsky spoke loudly, to ensure everyone could hear him. "Looks like the witness who lives behind this unit was right about the odd knocking sounds. The sick bastards must have hammered up a new shelf after each kill."

Russo glared at Brodsky, but the detective didn't give in. "It's a real shame the unis were called off this detail."

"Watch it," Blake growled.

Ignoring him, Brodsky continued, "Who was it who ordered that again? Oh, that's right. It was Russo. Tough luck there, Special Agent. I guess us local detectives aren't such bumbling hicks after all, huh?"

Everyone in the room collectively held their breath as Russo chewed over Brodsky's commentary. They expected the FBI agent to explode, but he decided to tackle this confrontation from a different angle.

"Fair enough, Brodsky. Now, why don't you pull your nose out of my ass and start sniffing around for the killers instead?"

Even Jones mentally conceded that Russo had done an admirable job of lobbying back Brodsky's serve, although he'd never admit that out loud.

Before Brodsky could say anything else, the Chief of Police spoke up gruffly. "Are you two cocks done crowing and pissing all over each other yet? If you don't mind, I'd like to catch these sickos before they kill another hen, thank you very much."

Russo walked away without a word.

"Sorry, Chief," Brodsky muttered.

* * * * *

Timothy Dellmond drove his ratty, spray-painted truck into the Hollows. Thanks to a big argument, Jennifer wasn't sitting next to him like usual.

Fuck her, he thought. *I can handle things just as well without her crazy ass.*

Despite this mental bravado, Timothy knew he'd never walk away from Jennifer. Their relationship was far from perfect, but he loved her. Plus, they knew each other's secrets, and there was way too much power in letting that type of information sneak away with an angry ex.

Timothy didn't pay much attention to the community while driving toward the back. He parked right on the line – *that'll teach that prick who thinks he owns the parking lot* – and turned off the truck.

His keys jingled as he hopped out of the vehicle and made his way down the sidewalk. Just before he slid his key into the apartment door's lock, he heard a noise from inside the unit. His entire body stiffened when he identified an unknown male voice.

If she's cheating on me, I'm going to kill both of them!

Timothy puffed out his chest and prepared to burst into the apartment. A fortuitously timed voice in the back of his head cautioned that it might be better to do a little reconnaissance first. He shoved his ear against the door and listened.

"Why is it taking so fucking long to get everything wrapped up? I could have cleared this place alone faster than this," a male voice roared.

Cleared this place? Oh, shit.

Timothy sunk to the ground and started crawling back down the sidewalk. As soon as he cleared the living room window, he stood up and ran. A heartbeat later, heavy footsteps burst free from his apartment. Realizing he might not make it, he grabbed his phone and yelled, "Siri! Send a text to Jennifer. We're busted. Run!"

Siri's voice issued a reply.

"Your text to Jennifer says 'we're busted. Run.' Would you like to send this now or edit it?"

"Send. SEND!"

Timothy's iPhone flew through the air as someone running with the force of a semi-truck body-slammed him to the ground. The phone's screen shattered as it landed in the parking lot.

At least there's that, Timothy thought with the hint of a smile.

A knee jammed his back as rough hands shackled him within a pair of horribly tight handcuffs.

"Stay down, fucker!" an officer shouted at him virulently.

That's a bit much, don't you think? Timothy mentally critiqued the unseen officer.

"Get on your fucking knees!" another voice barked.

Which one is it?

Before Timothy could ask for clarification, he was lifted into a kneeling position in front of his truck. A particularly upset officer pushed Timothy's face into the tailgate with brutal precision.

"Hey!" Timothy shouted. "That's brutality. I have rights, you know."

"Fuck you!" the officer responded before bouncing Timothy's face off of the tailgate for the second time.

Timothy's wallet was yanked free of his back pocket as a seemingly never-ending number of hands patted him down. One of the hands got more intimately acquainted with his crotch than Jennifer had been in weeks.

Damn perverts.

"It's definitely him, Chief."

A uniformed police officer handed Timothy's wallet to the chief, who then passed it to Russo. The FBI agent sauntered over to the man in cuffs with the same swagger as a cowboy at high noon.

"Timothy Dellmond?"

"Yeah?"

"You're under arrest."

CHAPTER THIRTY-THREE

"You're at a hotel? Why didn't you come stay with me?" Liz whined.

Anna held the phone a couple of inches from her ear in an attempt to minimize Liz's complaint. "I didn't want to bother you. Besides, my renter's insurance is paying for it. Plus, I know your husband isn't a fan of cats."

"Don't tell me you took the cats with you to the hotel?" Liz said.

"Of course, I did. What was I supposed to do, leave them behind?"

"They're cats, silly. They would have been fine in the apartment."

"Even if that's true, I didn't want to run the risk of them getting out when a contractor opens the door."

Anna was quickly losing patience with her sister, as usual. The two of them had such a different world view – and such drastically different priorities – that Anna sometimes wondered if they really were sisters.

Before Liz could launch into another complaint, her eye was caught by a 'breaking news' ticker at the bottom of the screen. "Wait, what?" she said to herself in a distracted tone.

"Huh?" Anna said.

"Turn on Channel 7. Now!"

Anna knew Liz well enough to know it would be pointless to ask any follow-up questions. It took a minute for her to locate the remote control and get the TV tuned to the right channel, but once she was there, her mouth fell open.

"We now go live to this breaking news alert with Diane Douglas," a man's voice said as the brief news ticker turned into an actual report.

"Thank you, Jake. We're live at the scene here at Corvo Hollows. Police say a suspect was arrested earlier today in connection with the serial murders that have rocked Metro Detroit in recent weeks. Although officers haven't released any information about the suspect yet, we do have a witness on hand. Can you tell us what you saw?"

The camera panned to Rene. Anna's hand flew to her mouth as she squeaked, "Oh, my god, it's Rene," before being shushed by her sister.

"I pulled into the parking lot and saw my next-door neighbor booking it down the sidewalk. I've never seen an older man run that fast. Then a big, burly officer jumped on top of him. It was the craziest thing I've ever seen," Rene said with a tremor of excitement in her voice.

"What can you tell us about your neighbor? And remember not to say his name for the time being," the reporter cautioned.

"Well, he hasn't lived here for very long. He and his girlfriend moved up here from Tennessee."

"Does his girlfriend live here, too?"

"Yes, but I haven't seen her today."

"Did you ever suspect he might be involved in something like this?"

"Honestly? No. I just thought he was a little weird. But another neighbor called this weeks ago. I'm pretty sure she told the cops, too. It's too bad they didn't take her more seriously. Might have saved some lives."

Diane's eyes lit up and she had to restrain herself from smiling. This was the type of scoop that could lead to awards and national opportunities if she played her cards right.

"It's certainly quite shocking to hear that some of the bloodshed may have been preventable," Diane said to Rene before turning to face the camera head-on. "We'll follow-up on this breaking news story, and the potential bombshell you just heard here first, as soon as more information becomes available."

Silence continued to dominate the phone line for a couple of beats before it was shattered by Liz's shrieking. "I knew that place was no good! You need to move, Anna. Come stay with me."

"Huh? No!" Anna replied. "I'm not moving. Besides, this could have happened anywhere. Crime has no address, remember?"

"Don't be so naive, sis. You *know* you live on the bad side of town."

"There is no bad side in a town like this."

"If there wasn't before, there definitely is now," Liz argued.

"I can't do this with you right now. I'll call you back later."

Anna hit 'end' on her phone before Liz could respond. She sat back in the hotel room chair, simultaneously shocked and vindicated by what she'd just heard.

It was them all along. I was right.

Lost in thought, Anna almost missed it when the news interrupted the next program. By the time she looked up, a police press conference was already underway.

"...time is of the essence, and we're asking for help from the entire community. If you see this woman or have any information about her whereabouts, please call the station at..."

A photo of Jennifer O'Neil appeared on the screen.

Oh shit.

Anna fretted over the possibility that her neighbor knew she'd gotten the police involved. Would Jennifer decide to come after her to tie up loose ends?

Anna's phone lit up with an incoming call. The number looked familiar, but she still hesitated before clicking the answer button.

"H-hello?"

"Anna? It's Detective Brodsky."

"I just saw the news," she blurted out.

"I'm sorry I didn't get a chance to call you earlier. I was hoping to give you a heads-up before the news plastered it everywhere."

"So, it's really them?"

"It appears that way, yes. I...we're concerned about your safety, Anna. O'Neil is still out there. We don't know for sure if she's connected the dots, but your encounters with them might have her..."

"I know," Anna interjected. "She might think I'm the one who ratted them out. Especially since I'm guessing they have no idea that their attic was flooded."

"Right," Brodsky confirmed. "Where are you right now?"

"I'm at a hotel. The one just down the street from Corvo Hollows."

"Okay, good. Stay put for now, and don't open your door for anyone until I get there. We'd like to move you to a safe house, okay?"

"Can my cats come?"

"What?"

"Can my cats come? They're here at the hotel with me and I can't leave them behind."

"Uh, sure. Yeah. Bring them along. What's your room number?"

"217."

"I'm on my way," Brodsky assured her.

CHAPTER THIRTY-FOUR

"Do you know why you're here?" Russo asked.

Timothy Dellmond looked around the small interrogation room. He spotted the cameras anchored on the walls and knew other law enforcement officers were peering in from the other side of the mirror.

Busted is busted, he sighed to himself. *Might as well get this over with.*

"Yeah, I take it you found my stash?" he said with a hint of hostility.

"Your stash? Is that what you two call it?"

Timothy twisted his wrists. The handcuffs were almost cutting off all the circulation to his fingers, and having them secured to the table via a chain wasn't make things any easier. To make matters worse, he'd had a persistent itch on the end of his nose for several minutes.

"I mean, yeah. Isn't that what *everyone* calls it?"

"You seem pretty nervous, Timothy. Why is that, exactly?"

Timothy looked at Russo like he had suddenly sprouted an extra head. Unable to keep his anger under control, he blurted out, "Why do you think, asshole?"

"Why do you keep trying to rub your face against your shoulder?" Russo asked.

"Because my damn nose itches, that's why!"

Russo slowly pulled a business card out of his wallet and sauntered over to Timothy as if he had all the time in the world. The two stared each other down as Russo stood above him. Finally, Russo rubbed the edge of the card up and down Timothy's nose a couple of times.

"Better?"

"Yes," Timothy replied in a calmer tone.

Russo sat back down across the table. "Good. Maybe now you'll start paying better attention to my questions."

The FBI agent's words hung in the air for a moment as he sized his opponent back up. *This doesn't look like a man with enough guts and forethought to pull off those killings. Maybe his girlfriend is the brains of the operation.*

"So, here's what I'm thinking, Timothy. I think maybe you got yourself in too deep because you fell in love with the wrong woman. Maybe Jennifer gets off on this sort of thing and you went along with it. Maybe you didn't think you had any other options. Or maybe she sucked you in so far, so quickly that you were afraid to end things with her. Does that sound about right?"

A quizzical expression altered Timothy's features. "What in the hell are you talking about, man?"

"I'm talking about your 'stash.' If Jennifer's the brains of this operation, now would be a good time to tell us that. Help us find her, and you might even get out of prison before you die."

Timothy did love Jennifer, but the thought of getting a reduced sentence greatly appealed to him. He allowed the idea of betraying her to spin around in his head for a bit. With each loop it made around his gray matter, the better the idea sounded.

"Okay, you got me. I wasn't going to say anything because what man likes to admit he's under some woman's thumb, right?"

Russo nodded along with a false display of manly comradery. "Exactly," the agent said. "It's embarrassing to let a bitch take the reins."

Timothy's eyes lit up. *This is a pig I can talk to. Might actually be worth his weight in bacon if he didn't have a damn badge.*

Any second now, Russo thought. *This idiot is going to give up everything to look like a tough guy.*

"You're right, though. She did take the reins. Made me feel weak. That's why I knocked her around sometimes. Couldn't let her have all the power in the relationship, you know?

Russo nodded and decided to egg Timothy on. "Oh, absolutely. Want to hear a secret?" he whispered while leaning in closer.

"Yeah, man," Timothy responded.

"I knock my wife around, too. When she deserves it. You know what I mean," Russo winked.

As usual, Russo felt absolutely zero shame about lying to a perp. His fictious wife had been everything from a saint to a cheating whore during the past decade. Whatever it takes to get a confession, he always said. Of course, that type of attitude – and the shitty thoughts that went along with it – were probably the major reason he'd never had a long-term relationship with anything other than his FBI badge.

Timothy's countenance made it clear that Russo had hit all the right buttons. Even though he didn't want to admit it to anyone, let alone himself, Timothy was impressed by this man. He even kind of liked him. Russo was the type of guy who could understand him. Under different circumstances, they could have been drinking buddies.

"How about you help me help you, friend?" Russo said with his trademark shit-eating grin.

"I'd like that," Timothy said. "What do you need to know?"

"Where's Jennifer? Tell me, and I can go pick her up. I'll let the judge know you cooperated. He listens to me, man. You'll get leniency."

The men on the other side of the one-way mirror had to put their hands over their mouths to avoid letting their laughter ruin Russo's work. "That's our smooth operator," Special Agent Blake whispered to the police chief. "He promises the world, and then pulls the rug out from under their feet. Works like a charm."

"I'm not one-hundred percent sure, but I can tell you the places she might be."

"That's a good start, Timothy."

"One thing, though."

"Anything."

"When you catch her, can I have a couple of minutes alone with her in this room?"

Russo's left eyebrow shot up. Timothy was showing more guts than he anticipated.

"Why's that, Timothy? Looking for one last lay?"

"No. Looking to get one last punch in for what she's done to me," Timothy replied in an almost convincing tone of contrition mixed with righteous anger.

"I'll see what I can do, friend," Russo said with a smile. As soon as Timothy gave him a few locations, he walked out of the room.

"Don't you think you took things a bit too far there, Russo?" Police Chief Brower asked. "That got really gross by the end. Can't say I condone such tactics."

Russo looked the man up and down before meeting his stare. "And that, Chief, is why your department fails. If you think you can catch monsters by prancing around like a prim and proper princess, you've got another thing coming."

Russo turned away, and Brower responded under his breath. "At least none of my guys are every bit as bad as the monsters, asshole."

CHAPTER THIRTY-FIVE

Anna attempted to get comfortable in the safe house, which was really nothing more than a small, two-bedroom home on the other side of town. Of course, no one outside of law enforcement knew she would be staying here, so that definitely gave it an edge over her apartment.

She opened the refrigerator and smiled. It was well-stocked with a nice variety of food. The freezer and cupboards gave her even more options. The kitchen, although small, had more than enough supplies to enable her to make a feast.

As a serving of fettucine noodles cooked, she finally allowed herself to begin processing the news; her neighbors had been caught. The murders were over, and she'd been vindicated. That wouldn't provide much in the way of solace to the victims' families, but she couldn't possibly overstate how big of a relief it was to know she wouldn't have to hear that crazy knocking anymore.

She'd been told that staying off of social media was a must, and she didn't want to try to work on any of her art projects while eating. Fortunately, she'd stuck her Kindle in her purse before heading to the hotel. It would now be her sole form of entertainment aside from a dusty collection of old DVDs that sat in the living room.

With a fork in one hand and a Kindle in the other, she dove deep into the world of a fictional thriller. All things considered, some might question her current choice of reading material – and she knew Brodsky would poke fun at her again for it – but getting lost inside a Mark Edwards story was exactly what she needed.

Her phone rang two chapters later, and she almost dropped her Kindle. Brodsky's words – *"promise me you won't answer the phone or open the door for anyone not in law enforcement"* – stuck out in her memory like a sore thumb as the temptation to answer Jaxon's call almost made her break her promise.

Guilt gnawed at her stomach as she allowed the call to go to voicemail. Jaxon and Rene would undoubtedly start wondering where she was soon, and she didn't want to worry them unnecessarily. Liz would demand answers soon, too, but that didn't bother her quite as much.

How long am I expected to hide? she wondered for the first time.

* * * * *

Russo and his partner, Blake, drove through the township's hot streets. Sun reflected off the FBI vehicle's windshield, and Russo swore as his vision all but vanished for a few seconds. His hand fumbled in the center console for sunglasses.

The darkness that settled over his eyes was barely good enough to prevent the evening sun from obscuring his vision again.

I hate summertime.

If Russo ever decided to be completely honest, he'd have to admit that he hated almost everything except for his job. He knew that others disliked his methods, but he also had the highest close rate in the entire Detroit FBI branch. Pretending to be a psychopath seemed like a small price to pay for getting the dregs of society off the streets.

Russo's lack of inner self-awareness stopped him from teetering off the ledge of his justifications and falling headfirst into his personal truth. The psych evaluation from earlier in his career didn't lie, though; he was much more than just a loose cannon. If his father hadn't been a decorated FBI agent, it's highly unlikely he would have been admitted into the Quantico Training Academy. Graduating with the top marks in his class also helped convince those in charge to ignore his less than savory traits.

The only viable difference between Russo and all the criminals he'd busted was that he never crossed the line from your average, everyday sociopath into a criminal psychopath. Instead, he channeled those urges into the tales he weaved during each interrogation.

He'd also never heard a little voice inside his head telling him that it was wrong to lie. If he hadn't possessed a cold, clinical view of the criminal system, he could have easily ended up on the other side of a badge.

Russo pulled into a handicapped spot at the movie theater where Timothy had last seen Jennifer. It was a long-shot at this point, but maybe she'd decided to take in a double-feature. He and his partner walked side-by-side up to the entrance with measured, purposeful strides. Their body language screamed that they thought they were more important than everybody else nearby.

An impatient driver honked her horn at them as they took their time crossing the parking lot. Blake's eyes flashed with anger. Before he could do anything regrettable, Russo said, "we've got better things to do."

Blake – who also benefited from having a family member in the FBI – had been assigned to Russo two years ago, and he was definitely a bit of a loose cannon. Blake's anger tended to flare up in confrontational situations, and he really enjoyed Russo's interrogation techniques. Between the two of them, they were a lawsuit waiting to happen.

But somehow, Russo managed to keep Blake's worst impulses in check. Blake's dogged loyalty to his partner – and gleeful joy at his rough edges – also helped show Russo where the line was. If Blake got too excited, Russo knew he needed to pull back a bit.

Russo and Blake walked into a crowd of people who were waiting in line to buy movie tickets. Frustrated, they cut straight to the front of the line.

"Hey, come on, man. Wait your turn like everyone else," a guy toward the front of the line grumbled.

Blake turned around, held up his FBI badge, and pointed to it. "Do you see this? It means I *always* go straight to the front of every line. Do you know why? Because this means I'm not a loser, unlike the rest of you."

Russo chuckled to himself. It wasn't smart to let Blake harass citizens like that, but he knew Blake needed to blow off some steam, too. If their boss – who they'd nicknamed the Boy Scout – was here, they'd both get chewed out. What he didn't know couldn't hurt them, though.

A sweaty-faced, nervous teenager behind the ticket counter said, "Can I help you?"

"Yeah," Russo responded while holding his badge up to the plexiglass between them for inspection. "I need to know if you've seen this woman today." He slid a photo of Jennifer O'Neil in the area usually reserved for tickets and payments.

"I think so? It's been several hours, though."

The boy showed the photo to a teen girl working at the next ticket window.

"She was here, all right, but she ran out a few hours ago," the girl said.

"She ran?"

"Yeah, like her hair was on fire. I figured it was some type of family emergency or something."

"Did you happen to see which direction she headed in?" Russo asked.

"She went out the door on the far right, but that's all I saw."

"Thanks," Russo said as he motioned for Blake to follow him back to the car.

"What do you think?" Blake asked as they clicked their seatbelts.

"She was on foot. Going right would take her toward the apartment, but none of the unis stationed there have reported anything. So, it stands to reason she stopped somewhere else on the way home. That or Timothy warned her somehow. Not sure why anyone would be dumb enough to head toward the source of trouble instead of away, though."

The two men left the parking lot in search of the next place on Timothy's list of possibilities.

Jennifer's chest sunk against the outside wall of the theater as she exhaled for the first time in more than a minute. The cocky stride of the two agents – combined with their dark sedan – had her convinced the cops were on her tail. She had left the inside of the theater hours ago, but she had no idea where else to go. After making a quick stop at the pizza place next door, she'd ducked behind the large multiplex cinema to strategize her next game plan.

She was relieved that Timothy had warned her. Otherwise, she might have stayed inside the theater until it closed out of spite. Today's argument between them had been especially rough, and she had the black eye to prove it. It was far from her first shiner, but she refused to label herself as a victim. After all, she'd dished out just as many bruises as he had over the years.

She knew they made most dysfunctional couples look completely functional by comparison, but that didn't change the simple fact that she loved him. And she knew her feelings weren't one-sided. The reality was that most of their physical fights had been the result of far too many drugs and sleepless nights. But just like with Timothy, she couldn't figure out how to kick her habit for good, nor was she sure she even wanted to.

I can't believe we've already blown it in Michigan.

They'd been chased out of several states already by the authorities getting way too close, but this was the first time either of them had been in custody with charges that would apparently stick. She knew she had no way of helping Timothy out of his current predicament. For the first time since receiving his text, she envisioned life without him.

Tears streaked down her rough cheeks. Several years ago, she'd still taken pride in her appearance. Now, she cared more about the drugs that left her with sallow skin, red bumps all over her body, brittle hair, and a smile that could no longer elicit favors from unsuspecting males.

I'm alone now, she sobbed as she crouched down against the building in an effort to remain as inconspicuous as possible. *And I need to get the hell out of here.*

Unsure exactly how to flee with limited cash, no vehicle, and no way to get her next fix, she resorted to an inspirational line from an old self-help audio book: *It's time to take matters into my own hands.* Thinking that and doing it were entirely different things, but it still provided her with a burst of very shaky confidence.

I'll wait it out until nighttime. Then, I'll head toward Dearborn.

It would be a long walk – probably four or five hours, if her mental calculations were right – but the Amtrak and Greyhound stations in Dearborn would be her best bet to disappear.

I hope I have enough money for a ticket.

CHAPTER THIRTY-SIX

Anna stared at her phone, willing it to stop ringing. Jaxon had called twice already, and now Rene's ringtone filled the silence of the safe house. Anna flipped her sound profile off in a bid to remove some of her guilt. If she couldn't hear them calling, she couldn't possible feel as bad about basically short-term ghosting on them, right?

As much as guilt and worry nagged at her, there was also another insidious worm wriggling through her brain. *Why did Rene and Jaxon claim they couldn't hear the knocking sounds? The sounds were real, after all. At least, I think they were always real.*

Unsure what else to do, Anna peaked through the living room curtains and spotted the reassuring presence of a police car. Brodsky had promised her that an officer would always be nearby until they took Jennifer O'Neil into custody.

If only my ex could see me now. He'd really think I was crazy, hiding out in a safe house, questioning the two people who clearly care more about me than anyone else in the world.

It wouldn't surprise me if I only imagined it when Jaxon was over. Wouldn't anyone start hearing scary sounds all the time if they lived next door to serial killers? As for Rene, I asked her to listen to a muddled recording in the middle of a loud restaurant. No wonder she couldn't make sense of what she heard.

Relieved at having worked out the puzzle, she stashed her phone in the other room. *Out of sight, out of mind.*

* * * * *

"Have any luck?" Jones asked Russo.

Russo's eyes shot daggers at the young detective. "Do you see me dragging a handcuffed perp through the office?"

Jones swallowed hard and shook his head.

"Then no, I didn't. Now get out of my way and stop asking stupid questions."

Jones stood aside and let the FBI agent pass. As a detective, he'd had a few encounters with the FBI. None of them had been as gruff as Russo, and Blake wasn't much better.

I'll be so happy when this case is over, Jones thought.

Brodsky walked into the station. "Hey, partner," he greeted Jones while handing the younger man a coffee.

Jones' face lit up. "Thanks!" The first sip was divine, and it reminded Jones that the entire world wasn't a dark cesspool filled with serial killers and angry FBI agents.

"Ahh. This is exactly what I needed. Thanks again, boss."

"You're welcome, Jughead."

Jones chuckled. Many of the other officers and detectives had taken to calling him Jughead on day one. Brodsky usually refrained, though. Although the nickname annoyed Jones in some ways, it felt good to have Brodsky take a lighthearted stab at him. Once again, he looked toward the silver lining that existed outside of the department. He liked his job, but it wasn't always easy to deal with so much darkness.

"Anything new on the docket?" Jones asked.

"Just trying to track down O'Neil. It's probably a bit of a longshot, considering she has no wheels, but I thought we'd head over to Dearborn and check out the train and bus stations."

The drive to each transit hub was uneventful. Brodsky and Jones informed the train and bus station employees about their search for Jennifer O'Neil and left a photo of her at both locations. Brodsky's statement about their short trip being a longshot had proven correct so far, but he still had a hunch that O'Neil might be headed to Dearborn. With nothing else to definitively go on, the two detectives decided to go home and get some much-needed sleep.

* * * * *

Jennifer shook with misery. It had been far too long since she'd scored, and she wasn't exactly making good time. Sighing, she sat down on a large, decorative rock next to the sidewalk.

Maybe just one more time...

She didn't want to do it without Timothy, but taking action once more should help her get enough money for a bump or two. She'd stick to the plan the two of them always used. It would still work. It *had* to work. She couldn't go on like this much longer.

* * * * *

The sun rose on yet another oppressively muggy day in Metro Detroit. The detectives, FBI agents, and Anna had all passed the night in varying states of sleep. Jennifer O'Neil had managed to stay off of everyone's radar long enough to get a fix.

An early jogger's leg muscles quivered as she pushed herself to cover more ground before work. She cut through a parking lot and ran up a small incline. Her reward was a tiny greenspace that provided a bit of shade.

The jogger's face barely had time to register a satisfied grin before she hit an unexpected slick spot that sent her careening through the air. The hard impact of her chest flattening against the merciless ground left her breathless and dazed for a moment.

She struggled to her knees and looked for the source of her misery. A rush of air flooded her lungs, but it didn't stay long as her scream split the air in two. Blood coated her white jogging shoes and powder blue track pants. A naked, disembodied female torso faced her from the base of a nearby tree.

* * * * *

Russo stormed into the interrogation room. In his anger, the agent didn't even bother to reach up and turn off the camera. As the red light flashed, he grabbed Timothy's head and bashed it against the table.

"You son of a bitch!" Russo roared.

Timothy's shocked face was newly adorned by a trail of blood.

"What the...?

Before he could finish his first thought, Timothy's head bounced off the table again.

"Where is she? WHERE IS SHE? You'd better give me the truth this time, asshole."

"Who? Jennifer? I told you everything I know."

Russo made a fist and reared his arm back.

"Whoa, whoa," Brodsky said as he rushed into the room and held Russo back. "I want to find her as much as you do, but this isn't the way to do that, man."

Russo broke free of the detective's grasp, spun around, and shoved Brodsky against the wall.

"What the fuck do you know? Can you lead me to his bitch?"

"No…"

"Then get the hell out of my way, you townie piece of shit, and let me do my job."

Russo's words stung. Every officer hated dealing with state and federal agents who looked at them as basically nothing more than incompetent, bumbling, Barney Fife wannabes. It wasn't fair or true; Brodsky had an excellent track record. But telling that to someone who wanted to look down on him wasn't going to do any good.

"You'd better listen closely if you don't want to end up with some broken bones, Dellmond," Russo barked as he pelleted Timothy's face with spittle. "While your dumbass is sitting here, your bitch is off her leash. She did it *again*. I guess she really doesn't need your help, you worthless piece of trash. Now tell me where the fuck she is before we pin all of this on *you!*"

Torn by concern for Russo's actions and Anna's safety, Brodsky opted to let the FBI agent handle matters in his own way. After all, it would be Russo's ass in a sling if Dellmond decided to lawyer up and press charges.

The phone rang five times before going to voicemail. Brodsky frowned as he hung up. *Maybe she's sleeping or in the shower?*

He called the uni next. "Is everything good on your end?"

"Yeah, no worries, Detective. I haven't seen anything out of the ordinary."

"Okay, good. Call or text me hourly with reports from now on. Got it?"

"Will do, sir."

Relieved, Brodsky slipped outside for a cigarette. When his phone rang a few puffs later, he eagerly pulled it out of his pocket, only to be met by his ex's number. Groaning, he shoved his phone back into its typical resting place.

This was Susie's third call. He knew he should get back to her, but he'd been way too busy with this case. *She should know that, dammit,* was his justification for ignoring her. The truth was that he cared far more about keeping an eye on Anna – even though she had a boyfriend – than he did about trying to reconcile things with the woman who loved him.

CHAPTER THIRTY-SEVEN

Guilt gnawed at Anna, and she finally gave into the overwhelming voice in her head that commanded she check her phone again. There was a missed call from Detective Brodsky, along with several more calls and texts from Rene and Jaxon.

She fired off a quick message to Brodsky – *"sorry I missed your call, all is good on my end"*– before scrolling through her other messages. One from Rene made every hair on her body stand on end.

"I'm not sure if you're mad at me or something, but please, PLEASE, at least let me know you're all right. There was another murder this morning. They won't say who the victim is. I'm so worried about you, Anna. Jaxon and I both are."

The world tilted slightly as Anna tried to absorb the meaning of Rene's words. Another murder had taken place, even with Timothy Dellmond behind bars. Could Jennifer O'Neil have acted alone? Was Anna next on her hitlist?

"Screw it," Anna said out loud as her fingers flew over the phone's keyboard. It was one thing to keep her location a secret, but it was entirely another to make her closest friend so worried about her.

"I'm okay, Rene. Sorry for scaring you. I'm not mad, either, not at you or Jaxon. The police put me up in a safe house and told me not to answer my phone for a few days. Please tell Jaxon not to worry."

Before she could put her phone down, the telltale bubbles of a reply message starting blinking on the screen.

"Thank God! I was so scared you were dead. Is there anyone else in the safe house with you?"

"No," Anna replied. *"Just a cop stationed outside."*

"You shouldn't be alone right now. Let me come over and help."

"I don't know...the detective said not to..."

"I'm not taking no for an answer. I'm sure the detective wouldn't mind someone else being there to help keep you safe. That crazy chick is still on the loose, after all."

Anna hesitated for a moment longer before giving in. Once Rene had the safe house's current address, she promised to rush right over.

"I'll be there in 30 minutes. Sit tight. The cavalry is coming, lol."

Anna knew she'd disregarded Brodsky's biggest rule of hiding in a safe house, but she was also secretly pleased that she would soon have company. Rene was right; it *had* been difficult doing all of this on her own.

The soft tread of another person's shoes against the laundry room's linoleum tile caught Anna's attention. "Officer?" she called out. This wouldn't be the first time he'd come in for a drink of water or a bathroom break. When he didn't respond, she decided she'd only imagined the sound.

She sat at the dining room table and soon became immersed inside her book again. Only ten minutes had passed since the last text from Rene, but Anna was completely wrapped up in discovering the identity of the bad guys. Just as these answers became clear, painful sparks shot through her head. She fell face forward on the table, oblivious to the intruder and their subsequent actions.

At the same time, Brodsky called the uni back. Seventy minutes had elapsed since the uni's last report, and it set the detective's teeth on edge. When the officer didn't answer his cellphone, Brodsky walked over to a CB unit and tried to contact the man via his police radio. Silence greeted him, and nothing more.

"Shit!" Brodsky grabbed his belongings while signaling for Jones. "Come on, we've got to roll right now!"

In most cases, the two kept their vehicle undercover. This time, Brodsky had Jones toss the flashing light on top so they could weave in and out of traffic more effectively. As the tires of their car squealed around the corner, they saw the cop car sitting in front of the safe house.

"If he's worried me for nothing..." Brodsky trailed off.

They parked haphazardly on the street, and Brodsky jumped out as he was still jamming the stick into park. He stomped to the driver's side window of the marked police car, huffing and ready to shout.

"What the hell, Offic..." the last word died on Brodsky's lips and the color drained from his face.

Jones glanced inside the vehicle, turned around, and said, "Jesus," while trying to keep his emotions in check.

"Call it in," Brodsky yelled as he ran toward the house. The frantic cries of "officer down, officer down," faded into the background as his feet hit the pavement. He unholstered his gun and disengaged the safety mechanism before kicking the backdoor wide open.

"Police!" he barked authoritatively. A small pool of blood grabbed his attention, and he fought to keep his panic under control. *Gotta secure the house first,* Brodsky reminded himself. Auto-pilot kicked in long enough for him to investigate every room. Whoever had been here was long gone, and they'd taken Anna with them.

He stumbled outside with tears blurring his vision. "Fuck!" He kicked a trashcan so hard it flew halfway through the back yard. He crouched down, pressed his back against the side of the safe house, and pinched the bridge of his nose.

How could this have happened? We were so careful.

A car door shutting broke his concentration. Brodsky rushed back to the street in time to see Rene sauntering down the sidewalk. Unsure what to think, he aggressively yelled, "Stop right there! Put your hands up, Rene!"

"What?" she balked, confused. Once she noticed a gun pointed at her, self-preservation kicked in enough for her to comply with the detective's commands.

Jones ran over and secured Rene while Brodsky checked her for weapons. Coming up empty, Brodsky grilled her with a series of rapidly fired questions.

"What are you doing here? How did you know to come here? Do you know where Anna is?"

"Whoa, back up, Officer. I can only answer one question at a time."

"Fine. And it's *Detective*, dammit. Tell me why you're here."

"Anna told me I could come over. She's gotten quite lonely sitting in that safe house all by herself, you know. Maybe you should keep her company." Rene suggested flirtatiously.

"Cut the crap, Rene. We don't have time for it. Anna's missing. What do you know about that?"

The nonplussed expression that changed Rene's face convinced Brodsky that Rene either knew nothing or was the world's best liar. Considering how overtly – and poorly – she flirted, he guessed it was the former.

"Oh my god. She's missing? Is she okay?"

"I wish I knew, Rene."

"Wasn't there a cop guarding her?"

"He's...he didn't make it."

"You mean he's *dead?* Oh no...no, no, no." Tears streaked down Rene's face as the implications of everything she'd heard in the past few minutes hit home. "Don't just stand there," she screeched. "You have to find her!" Rene's fists collided again and again against Brodsky's shoulders as she continued to scream "find her, find her, find her!"

As the adrenaline transformed from anger to sorrow, Rene sagged against Brodsky, who caught her by her elbows and held her up. "I'm going to find her, if it's the last thing I ever do," he vowed.

An ambulance raced down the street, followed quickly by several officers, detectives, and FBI agents. They were all too late to help Officer Freeham, whose shoddily amputated left hand had accelerated the blood loss from his other injuries.

Rene agreed to go to the station with another detective duo and instantly complied when the tech team asked her for her cellphone.

"Your text messages might give us some clues," they'd told her.

"I don't really see how, but of course," she said while sliding her phone across the table. "Anything at all, if you think it could help. Wait...you don't think those messages were, like, hacked or something, do you?"

"It's hard to say right now, ma'am, but we're definitely going to check out every possibility," the tech answered.

"Please find my friend," Rene pleaded. "I'd just die if anything happened to her. Especially if it was my stupid fault for texting her."

"I don't know how I'm going to tell Jaxon," she muttered after the tech walked away.

* * * * *

"So, you're telling me she was not only dumb enough to give someone her location but she also managed to get herself kidnapped?"

Brodsky silently counted to ten to avoid giving into Russo's goading.

"It's pretty convenient, though, isn't it?" Russo continued.

"What is?"

"The officer getting killed and Anna disappearing right after she told someone where to find her."

"The techs have already confirmed that Rene's phone pinged towers all the way to the safe house. She was nowhere near it until after everything went down."

"Sure, but that's not what's bothering me, Brodsky."

"Then what...?"

"I'm still not entirely convinced that your little crush isn't involved in some way."

"Seriously? This crap again?"

Russo stepped closer to Brodsky. Standing nose to nose, the FBI agent said, "Yup," placing a special emphasis on the last letter. He then turned at the heel and stalked off, leaving the detective reeking of anger.

The Chief poked his head into the room, took one look at Brodsky, and said, "For the love of god, what is it this time?"

"His theories are ridiculous."

"Perhaps..." Chief Brower responded as he absentmindedly stroked his chin. "But he still has one of the best close rates in the entire FBI. Maybe you should consider asking *why* he's gnawing on his Anna theory instead of dismissing him outright. You never know."

Biting his tongue, Brodsky gave Brower a curt nod and left the station. He wasn't going to believe the worst about Anna, no matter how hard Russo or the Chief pushed. He knew in his gut that he wasn't wrong about her.

CHAPTER THIRTY-EIGHT

Jaxon sat in the same interrogation room that had held Timothy Dellmond the day before. His eyes shied away from the harsh overhead lighting and focused on a softball-sized, rust-colored stain on the carpet instead.

Is that blood?

Russo and Blake were on the opposite side of the table. Jaxon wasn't handcuffed, but he got the impression that the FBI agents were looking for any reason to take him into custody.

Sighing internally, Jaxon remembered that most crimes against women were carried out by their significant other. No wonder they were giving him such a hard time. Never mind the fact that he'd willingly gone to the police station and had sat here answering their questions as patiently as possible for more than an hour now.

"Let's go over this one more time," Russo said.

Frustrated, Jaxon had to bite his lip to keep from making a snarky reply.

"Tell me about the last time you spoke to Anna."

"Like I said, it was a few days ago. She didn't answer any of my texts or calls after that Dellmond guy was arrested. I now know she was in a safe house, but I was worried sick. Rene filled me in on everything that happened after that." Unable to resist the urge any longer, he let his real thoughts slip. "I can't say I'm too impressed with your idea of a safe house, by the way. How the hell did this happen?"

"We ask the questions. You answer. Got it?" Blake sneered. "What do you keep staring at the floor for, anyway? Feeling guilty?"

"No, I'm *not*. There's a weird stain. Right there, see it?" Jaxon pointed. "Looks almost like blood."

"It *is* blood," Blake said with the hint of a ghoulish smile. "That's what happens when people don't cooperate."

In that moment, Jaxon finally recognized the pheromonal odor that filled the room. It was the type of stink that only bullies and other sociopaths emit.

I'm locked in a room with two crazy guys.

Before panic could set in, the Chief of Police entered the room.

"Gentlemen, I need to speak to you outside for a moment."

Grumbling and tossing Jaxon a threatening look, the two men stalked out of the room and let the door slam shut behind them.

"We have to let him go, you know," the Chief said.

"One more hour," Russo answered.

The Chief removed his glasses and wiped the sweat away from both sides of his nose. "Okay," he replied in a pained tone. "One more hour. But keep it clean, you hear me? And after that, if you still don't have a reason to charge him, you have to cut him loose."

* * * * *

Anna sat up groggily and experienced a twinge of pain in her wrists.

What the...?

She opened her eyes but was met by darkness. A cloth rubbed against her fluttering eyelashes. Cold steel pressed into the flesh of her wrists and reminded her of handcuffs.

A tremor shook her body as she struggled to understand what had happened. The last thing she remembered was reading a book at the safe house.

"Hello?"

An echo responded, making her current unknown location seem empty and cold. "Is anyone there?"

She tried to stand up, but her restraints wouldn't allow it. Every joint in her body ached. She didn't know how much time had passed, but her joints claimed she'd missed at least one or two doses of her fibromyalgia medication.

A panicked whimper started in the back of her head, and it took all of her mental fortitude not to start blubbering in the darkness.

Did Jennifer O'Neil catch me? Oh god, no. Please, no. I don't want to die.

Tears formed against her will and soon soaked the inside of the blindfold. She longed to dry her cheeks and blow her nose. She couldn't decide what was scarier; the fact that no one had answered her questions or the thought of someone else's voice echoing through the void in response.

The gut-churning fear and lack of light made Anna lose all sense of time. When she finally heard footsteps coming her way, she had no idea if it had been a few minutes or a few hours since she awoke.

"Hello?"

Silence.

"I heard you walking. Please say something."

Thick air hung over the room, and Anna was certain someone else had entered. After what seemed like an eternity, the footsteps slowly returned. The proof of another person's presence echoed off the walls with an increasing insistence, and Anna knew they were approaching.

Shit, shit, shit. I don't want to die, Anna's mind screamed as the harsh sensation of acid reflux filled the back of her throat.

A foreign object pressed against her lips. For half-a-second, she feared a sexual assault. Water started to spill off her unopen lips, and she opened her mouth to greedily suck in as much as possible. Dehydration had turned her mouth into the Sahara. Her stomach also complained loudly about being empty.

She thought she heard the slightest hint of a chuckle as her stomach rumbled. *Was that a woman?* It was impossible to tell.

"Please say something. Anything. Please?"

Although she'd been robbed of her vision, Anna could almost feel the air moving as the person shook their head no. A finger pressed against Anna's lips, and she took that as a command to be quiet. Holding back the urge to scream, she sat silently with her abductor. Questions flooded her head, but she resisted the urge to speak again.

What do you want? Are you going to hurt me? Where am I?

Her hair moved as someone gently stroked a few strands off her forehead. The gesture seemed almost tender somehow, but this accelerated the adrenaline coursing through Anna's veins. Afraid once again of being raped, a fresh batch of tears stained her face and soaked through the blindfold.

A tissue was placed around her nose. She could tell by the person's insistent pressing on both nostrils that they wanted her to blow her nose.

This makes no sense. What type of murderer helps someone blow their nose before offing them?

Food hit her lips, and she gratefully parted them again. The second it hit her tongue, she was relieved to discover it was a wedge of cheddar cheese. By the time cheese wedges stopped being popped into her mouth, she had her first darkly sardonic thought of the day. *Good food, water, and a gentle touch. Take away the whole being kidnapped thing, and this would almost be a good first date.*

She didn't actually believe that, but giving in to her own dark humor helped her feel more in control of the situation.

CHAPTER THIRTY-NINE

"Looks like Anna's got a bit of a dark side," Russo said to Brodsky and Jones.

"What do you mean?" Brodsky asked.

"Turns out her computer has some very interesting artwork on it. Including a drawing of disembodied heads and hands that she created *before* anyone knew that our killers were keeping a hand from each male vic."

Brodsky stared at Russo impatiently. "And your point is?"

"My point is that's a bit too coincidental for my taste. I told you before, and I'll tell you again; I don't believe she's innocent in all of this. Not by a long shot."

"You know she didn't kill..."

"I'm going to stop you right there. I never said she killed anyone. But that doesn't mean she's entirely innocent, either. Maybe she's been in on it the whole time. Maybe there was a rift between her and the killers that made her decide to rat them out. Who knows?"

Brodsky pinched the bridge of his nose as a reminder to not fly off the handle. "That's specious reasoning at best, and you damn well know it, Russo."

"Do I? We've got Dellmond in a holding cell and no one has seen Jennifer. So, tell me how she managed to kill a cop and kidnap someone in the middle of a populated suburban street. This isn't Detroit, Brodsky. The people here would report seeing something like that."

But not in Detroit because they'd have to deal with a prick like you, right? Brodsky thought.

"Have you even gotten Dellmond to admit to the murders yet?"

"He admitted to having his little 'stash' at the apartment, yes."

"Wait...you mean he *hasn't* actually owned up to the murders?"

"In a matter of speaking, yes."

Jones surprised everyone by opining, "That sounds like a fancy way of saying no to me, what do you think, boss?"

Oooh, well-played, kid, Brodsky thought while biting back a laugh.

"What, you think because you finally hit puberty that your balls are big enough to play in the big leagues now?" Russo sneered.

"Actually, I think your juvenile insults are a way of avoiding the question."

Brodsky looked at Jones with newfound respect. He hadn't known the younger detective had it in him.

"Whatever," Russo sputtered and walked away.

As soon as the FBI agent was out of hearing range, Brodsky offered Jones a high-five. "I'm impressed, Jones. You've got some brass ones today."

"I can't stand to listen to his superior tone, you know?"

"Yeah, I hear you. Now, how about we get out there and find Anna?"

* * * * *

Anna jerked awake. Disoriented, it took a moment for her to remember her current situation. She found it hard to believe she'd managed to fallen asleep on her own while blindfolded and handcuffed in an unknown place.

Did they spike my water with sleeping pills?

She tried to stretch and almost screamed from the pain that erupted through her joints and muscles. If she went much longer without her meds, it would no longer matter if the opportunity to flee presented itself as she wouldn't be able to run.

Anna took several deep breaths and tried to placate her nerve endings by shifting into a better position. She also concentrated on picking up any sounds, but was left disappointed. A fullness in her ears made her pretty sure that earplugs were blocking her hearing.

"Hello?" she experimented. Anna's distorted voice confirmed her theory. Unexpectedly, a straw was shoved between her lips. The gentle approach from before had clearly been abandoned for a rougher technique, but she still gratefully slaked her thirst.

"Can I have some more food, please?" she asked.

A heartbeat later, her head reeled to the side under the impact of a sharply delivered slap. Rough hands pulled her head back to the center and pried her mouth open before tossing some popcorn at her.

Despite her heart thudding from the physical assault, she played along with her captor's game by attempting to catch each thrown piece of popcorn in her mouth. Her efforts were considerably hindered by her lack of vision and hearing, but she managed to crunch down on quite a few popped kernels.

The unknown person in the room grew tired of the game before Anna had her fill. Unwilling to provoke their anger again, she sat quietly and prayed for another drink of water.

"Are you thirsty?" she heard from a deep, fierce voice that sounded miles away.

"Yes," she nodded.

"Drink up," the man said cruelly while tossing a glass of water in her face.

Anna had parted her lips in anticipation of the straw returning. Some of the precious fluid made it in to her mouth. Her body also trembled under the unexpected drenching. *Why are you doing this?*

* * * *

Chief Brower roared into Brodsky's office, which was currently occupied by Russo and Blake.

"What is this I hear about you not even mentioning the murders to Dellmond yet?"

"Hello to you, too," Russo responded tersely. The FBI agent stood up to gain a height advantage over the Chief. Blake imitated his partner's pose, right down to the crossed arms and indigent expression.

"Cut the bullshit, Russo. You can't keep a suspect locked up in my station for this long without following procedure, dammit!"

"Actually, yes, I can. Or have you forgotten your place? You might be the Chief of Police, but we're FBI, and we're calling the shots now."

Brower's face burned red. He *hated* working with the feds, especially hotshots like these two who thought they were above the law and superior to everyone.

"Just tell him before he lawyers up and we both lose him."

As Brower walked away, Russo decided to call Dellmond back into the interrogation room. He didn't like having his methods questioned, but it probably was time to move past the innuendo.

Maybe that would jar Dellmond enough to provide a few essential details.

Two officers practically carried Dellmond into the room and slammed him down on the hard metal chair before securing his handcuffs to the table. The suspect's head drooped forward. His greasy hair, stubbly face, and stained shirt all spoke of a man who was about to break.

"Tell me about your stash again," Russo began.

Dellmond's face lifted just enough for Russo to see his eyes were bloodshot and filled with tears. "I don't know what else you want me to say, man. Like I told you before, our stash was in the apartment. I know the cops found it, so what else do you need out of me?"

"For starters, why did you do it?"

Dellmond blinked uncomprehendingly. "Why?"

"Yes, why. W-H-Y," Blake spelled out with utter condescension.

"I know what the word why means," Dellmond mumbled.

"Then answer the fucking question!" Blake slammed his fists on the table mere inches from Dellmond's hands.

Dellmond jumped in surprise but only succeeded in chaffing his handcuffed wrists.

"I'm going to ask you one more time. Why did you do it?" Russo said.

"We needed money."

"So, what...you were robbing them? Or were these contract hits?"

"What?" Dellmond asked with terrified confusion. "I don't understand? I mean, yeah, we sold most of it. Kept some for ourselves, too," he admitted. "Never robbed a buyer, though."

"You sold human body parts? To who?"

Dellmond's stunned countenance set Russo's nerves on edge. He'd seen a lot of people lie about a lot of things, but this man truly looked surprised and confused.

"Body parts? No, man. Drugs."

"Do you expect us to believe that crap?" Blake said before Russo held up a hand to stop his partner.

Russo took a deep breath, wiped the bottom half of his face, and leaned across the table. He met Dellmond's eyes and asked, "Who committed the murders, Timothy? Was it you or your lady?"

"M-Murders? I don't know what you're talking about. We didn't kill nobody."

As much as he wanted to launch himself across the table and pummel Dellmond until he got a confession, Russo began to believe he'd actually screwed up.

I guess there's a first time for everything, he thought.

"So, what, we're just supposed to believe this prick?" Blake laughed. "Newsflash, Dellmond. Scum like you lie every single day. But you're not going to get away with. Isn't that right?" he asked Russo.

"Yeah," Russo responded without any enthusiasm. He went to the door, pounded twice, and yelled "we're done" before making a beeline for the parking lot.

If he really didn't do it, then who did? Maybe he's just covering for O'Neil?

CHAPTER FORTY

"We're live on the scene in Canton as local community members join the police in a citywide search for missing resident Anna Collins. Anna was last seen almost 24 hours ago, and local authorities are concerned she may have become the latest victim of the Body Snatcher," Diane Douglas said while staring into the news camera.

"Ugh," Brodsky grunted, just out of sight. Unwilling to hear any more of the reporter's spin on this particular case, he walked away toward the hastily erected coffee and donuts station. Jones followed him, knowing that his partner didn't want to talk, but probably shouldn't be alone, either.

The snacks sat near the beginning of the Lower Rouge Trail. Jones shoved half a powdered jelly donut in his mouth to fill the awkwardness as Brodsky meticulously prepared a cup of coffee he didn't even want. The two had been assigned to head this search, and Jones could tell Brodsky wasn't up for the task. Brushing the powder off his lips, Jones cleared his throat and picked up the megaphone.

"Can I have your attention, everyone?"

His voice hadn't become amplified as expected, and only a handful of people turned toward him. Jones looked at the megaphone as if it had betrayed him before turning crimson red; he'd forgotten to turn it on.

He flipped the switch and a loud squeal emitted from the megaphone. Swallowing hard, he tried to appear professional while repeating himself.

"Can I have your attention, everyone?"

The entire crowd hurried toward Jones. Most of the chatter died away as he spoke again.

"You all know why we're here. We're going to start canvassing this section of the Lower Rouge Trail in five minutes. We ask that you never stray more than an arm's length away from the person on either side of you. Keep your eyes peeled and watch the ground very carefully. If you see something that looks odd or out of place – anything at all – stop, raise your right arm, and call out. Are there any questions?"

A low buzz of chatter erupted as people turned to their friends and neighbors to clarify what they'd just heard.

"I've got a question," an angry voice rang out.

"Yes, ma'am?"

"How the hell could you let this happen to my sister?"

Jones grimaced. This could be the start of a public relations nightmare. He motioned for a uni to separate Liz from the crowd before joining her.

"I'm really sorry, ma'am. We're doing the best we can to find her."

"Bullshit. If it wasn't for your lot, she wouldn't even be missing! She was in your care when this happened, after all, instead of being with family, like she should have been."

"I understand your frustration," Jones began.

"Has your sister ever gone missing with a serial killer on the prowl?"

"No..."

"Then no, you don't, dammit! And you made me find out about it from the news. Don't you have any decency?" Liz cried.

"We'll find her," Jones said with a sense of finality. "Now, please, we have to get the search started."

Jones walked back to the front of the crowd. "We're going to start in a minute. Are there any other questions?" He held his breath, hoping there wouldn't be another confrontation.

Rene's voice stood above everyone else's as she shouted, "What exactly do you mean by something odd?"

"That's a good question, ma'am. We're looking for anything that could be connected to the missing woman. A shirt, a necklace, a dropped pack of gum, etc."

Rene nodded her understanding and put her head on Jaxon's shoulder.

"I can't believe this is happening," she whispered.

"I know," he replied hoarsely. He wrapped his arms around Rene and they held on to each other until Jones announced the official start of the search party.

Brodsky and Jones went to the center of the front line. Police officers flanked volunteers, and they lined up in a staggered series of rows that ensured no area would go untouched.

The vibrant greenery of the trail would have been inviting on any other day. Michigan's typically brutal summer weather had taken pity on them that day, and a soft breeze whispered through the leaves. The repeated footsteps of people on – and off – the manmade trail joined the wind in creating a soundtrack that Brodsky knew would haunt his dreams.

"I found something!" an astonished voice cried out. Jones stopped to mark their location, but Brodsky didn't hesitate. His long legs broke into a run as he rushed toward something that brought him hope and fear.

"What is it?" Brodsky huffed.

Anna's therapist, Jeani, pointed toward a thin zip-up hoodie. The impact of seeing a familiar item punched Brodsky with such force that his knees buckled. Jones stepped up with barely enough time to help his partner stay upright.

"It's hers," he murmured to Jones, who immediately turned to the closest uni. "Bag it and tag it, and be sure to write down the coordinates."

Turning the megaphone on again, Jones told the crowd of helpers they'd all be on the move again in a few minutes.

"It's okay to go home, boss. I know this one is personal for you."

Brodsky looked into Jones' eyes and seemed to consider his partner's suggestion before shaking his head no. Jones didn't try to change Brodsky's mind; it was abundantly clear that the matter was settled. Jones was pretty sure he wouldn't have been able to leave either if the shoe was on the other foot.

The next thirty minutes passed uneventfully. A few potentially suspicious items were discovered, but none of them were familiar to Brodsky. The search party moved at an agonizingly slow pace, and Brodsky barely restrained himself from moving ahead of the group.

An odd hush fell over the left side of the search party, as if they were collectively holding their breath. Brodsky's head hadn't finished turning in their direction when a chorus of screams and shouts ripped him free of his assigned spot yet again.

Don't be her, don't be her, don't be her. One thing was certain; whoever or whatever had elicited such a reaction from the volunteers wasn't going to be a happy discovery.

Coming to the same conclusion, Jones kicked his stride into high gear. He needed to get there before Brodsky. He wanted to protect him, somehow, from whatever gruesome sight awaited them.

The two pulled even and then stopped short as they took in the traumatized crowd. Even a couple of unis looked sick, and one had been unable to hold back tears.

"Stay here, Brodsky. I've got this," Jones said.

Brodsky's visage crumbled as the implication of Jones' words sunk in. "Is it her?" he croaked.

"I'll find out and be right back. Wait here," Jones said.

Dreading the moments to come, Jones had to mentally cajole his legs into moving forward. No matter what, he knew he had to see this through, for his partner and for Anna.

A circle of unis surrounded the unseen object that had caused so much uproar. Volunteers were being led away with shell-shocked expressions and tear-stained cheeks. He heard his partner's question echoed in countless whispers. "Is it her?"

He broke through the uni formation and sucked in his breath. Blood painted the grass and had spattered across several nearby trees and large rocks. In shock, Jones couldn't filter his brain's instant response. *Looks kind of like a Jackson Pollock painting.*

The officers waited for him to make a move. As one-half of the commanding team, Jones had to tell them how to proceed. His tremulous voice ordered them to call in the rest of the forensics team, along with notifying Russo and Blake. He also asked a couple of officers to sit with Brodsky until the vic's ID could be ascertained.

A woman's wailing broke his concentration as a crime scene photographer's flashbulb illuminated everything. Jones caught a flurry of movement from the corner of his eye before a uni caught Rene in his arms.

"I'm sorry, ma'am, but you can't go past here. I need you to back up, please," the young uni, fresh out of the academy, said with about as much force as a newborn kitten.

Jaxon stepped up with tears in his eyes, but an otherwise stoic expression. "Come here, Rene. I've got you," he said with his arms extended. The uni helped facilitate the exchange, and Rene found herself being slowly pulled backward by Jaxon.

At the same time, Liz tried to bully her way past the barricade of officers. She started to slip through, and then fell to her knees.

Jones approached the headless body. *Is this Anna?* Her body type seemed somewhat right, but he couldn't be sure. Pulling on a pair of latex gloves, he crouched next to the body, looking for any clues. A thin strap peeked out from underneath the victim's torso.

Enlisting the help of the strongest-looking uni, Jones lifted the body enough to free the small purse that had been laying beneath the small of her back. *That had to be uncomfortable,* Jones thought before blushing at the realization that nothing is uncomfortable when you're dead.

He slipped his gloved hand inside the purse and instantly hit pay dirt; her wallet slid into his grasp. Steeling himself, Jones flipped the wallet open and gasped. "Secure the perimeter," he muttered while stumbling out of the crime scene.

Brodsky spotted Jones and broke into a run, terrified that his partner's stunned countenance would come with a very steep price.

Brodsky almost slammed into Jones in his rush for answers. "What is it?" he demanded.

"Come over here," Jones gestured.

The two walked about twenty paces away from the rest of the crowd.

"Is it her?" Brodsky's voice raised an octave.

Jones flipped the wallet back open and held it out for Brodsky's examination. At first, the detective found it difficult to interpret what he was seeing. The name he expected to see was missing from the driver's license in front of him. Jennifer O'Neil stood in its place.

CHAPTER FORTY-ONE

"What the hell is going on with this case?" the Chief barked.

"Don't you dare talk to me like that," Russo responded, but with less bite than usual.

"This is *my* department, Russo. And your colossal fuck up is going to drag my name through the mud, not yours. Do you know what the media vultures are going to do with this? Dammit!"

"Has the lab confirmed the identity yet?"

"What?"

"Have we got a definite confirmation yet? It *is* still possible the ID is nothing more than a fake out until we know for sure."

Chief Brower considered this possibility, then shook his head. "We'll have it within an hour or two."

"Okay, good. Then we have at least another hour or two to break Dellmond."

"Technically...yes. But I've got to say that it really seems like you're grasping at straws here."

"Let me do my job, and I'll let you do yours," Russo answered gruffly.

I hate that guy, Brower thought.

Less than an hour later, Brower's door vibrated under someone's knuckles.

"Come in," he called out.

"We've got the report back, sir."

"And?"

"It's her, sir. The victim's definitely O'Neil."

"Thank you."

Brower leafed through the preliminary reports. Everything appeared to be in order. Sighing, he stood up, pushed his thinning hair back, and went to stop the mockery of an interrogation taking place down the hall.

He raised a loose fist toward the door, but decided at the last second not to knock. The door pushed open silently, and he saw a spectacle that would surely come back to haunt him.

Blake's hands were grasping the front of Dellmond's shirt. The FBI agent's nose pressed firmly against Dellmond's, and Russo stood by with a smirk.

"Tell us what you did, asshole!" Blake said before rearing one of his hands back to deliver a blow. Before the newly formed fist could locate its intended target, Chief Brower sprung into the room and pushed the agent backward.

"What the hell is going on in here?" Brower demanded.

"It's called an interrogation," Blake responded snidely.

"Yeah, well, your *interrogation* is over."

"On whose authority?" Russo challenged him.

"Mine! I don't care if you are FBI, you're making a travesty of this case, and you're doing it inside my house. Outside, gentlemen. NOW!"

Surprised by his forcefulness, Russo motioned for Blake to follow him. Blake's face dropped as he realized his moment of fun was over. Nothing made him happier than roughing up a bad guy; getting a confession was merely the icing on the cake.

"The results are in," Brower said. "Looks like you lose this round, Russo. It's definitely O'Neil."

The Chief's words made Russo doubt himself uncharacteristically. His instincts had never failed him before. How could they have let him down now?

"We have to cut Dellmond loose," Brower said.

"What? Come on, man. He's admitted to drug selling. And there were *heads* in his *attic,*" whined Blake.

"Yeah, heads that don't have any of his DNA or fingerprints on them. None of O'Neil's, either. And they're inside an attic that the two haven't been in possession of for more than a couple of weeks."

"What about a copycat killer," Russo began, in a desperate attempt to preserve his long streak of successful cases.

"No. Because here's another surprise for you, hotshot. We finally heard back from the gas station listed on O'Neil's receipt. They have security footage that proves Dellmond and O'Neil were nowhere near Michigan when the first murder happened. It's not them. And unless you have the drugs in your possession, we'll never make that charge stick, either. Now let him out before he sues us all into an early retirement."

Russo spun around angrily. He started to shout an expletive, but it died on his lips as the sight of Brodsky ignited a new idea. "Come on," he said to Blake and headed for the parking lot.

* * * * *

In Russo's absence, Brodsky and Jones were given the unenviable task of not only letting Dellmond go but of telling him about O'Neil.

"Jennifer's...d-dead?"

"I'm sorry, Mr. Dellmond," Brodsky said with a heavy heart. He couldn't help but wonder if O'Neil would still be alive if Dellmond hadn't been wrongfully arrested.

"A-and I can go? Just like that?" Dellmond asked as he choked down a sob.

"Yes, Mr. Dellmond. You're free to go. But I have to advise you that your apartment is still off-limits. Is there someone you can stay with? Or someone we can call for you?"

Dellmond's blurry, tear-filled eyes couldn't focus. Brodsky's words fell flat, but the most important message got through: don't go home.

"I-I'll figure something out," Dellmond mumbled as the detectives walked him to the exit door.

"Your truck is still at the Hollows, sir. Would you like a ride to it?" Jones asked softly.

"Huh?"

"Your truck. Would you like me to take you to it?"

"Y-yeah. That sounds good," Dellmond said in a daze. He'd already begun mentally flagellating himself over the fight that tore Jennifer from his side. If he hadn't hit her again...if he'd asked her to stay in the truck...would she still be alive?

"Wait a second," Brodsky said. "Before you leave, I have to ask you one thing, okay?"

Dellmond barely nodded through his grief.

"We know you weren't killers. But why did Jennifer try to get into your neighbor's apartment a few weeks ago?"

"Oh, that? Jennifer was tripping balls that day," Dellmond almost smiled as if he was taking a happy trip down memory lane. "She thought she'd be able to talk her way in and find something worth pawning. She wasn't a saint, you know? She did...we both did some stuff I'm not proud of for money. But she didn't deserve to die," he finished with the slight hint of mirthfulness wiped clean of his hallowed expression.

* * * * *

Russo and Blake let themselves into the dark, empty apartment. Their flashlight beams captured dust motes floating in the air. For a place full of furniture that had recently been lived in, it sure seemed dead, mused Russo.

Maybe that's because its seen death.

Following his latest hunch, Russo led Blake into the laundry room. A chain hung above their heads. Blake tugged it, and a ladder descended from the ceiling. Russo climbed the rickety steps first, careful not to put too much weight on any single part of the weak wood. Relief filled his lungs once he was no longer reliant on the ladder for safety.

His flashlight cast strange beams of light and shadow across the attic. Would anything be here? Or had his usually impeccable instincts let him down again?

"Russo!" Blake implored his partner. "Look!"

The beam from Blake's flashlight illuminated a gruesome discovery that brought a twisted smile to Blake's face. "Gotcha," he whispered and moved in for a better look.

"Call it in, Blake."

Russo walked away from the prize and examined the attic walls. His fingertips brushed against several pieces of wood until one gave slightly beneath his light touch. Excited, he placed the flashlight into his armpit and felt the panel in question more closely. At first, it didn't want to reveal its secret. But then a quick knock on the panel returned a hollow sound.

It's empty!

His hands dug around the sides of the panel until they found two loose screws. Digging into his pocket, he removed a Swiss Army knife. The screwdriver attachment made short work of the screws; only two full twists on each side allowed the loose panel to pull free of the wall.

"It's an access panel," Russo called to his partner.

Blake's heavy stride approached, and they shined their flashlights inside. "I bet it goes to the next attic."

The two men crouched down and entered the small space. Three feet in front of them stood another panel, but this one merely rested against the wall. They pushed it to the side and found themselves inside Timothy Dellmond's attic.

"Bingo," Russo said as Anna's attic behind them came to life with local officers and detectives.

"Shit," the FBI agents heard Jones say.

The two agents walked back into the now crowded attic sitting above Anna's apartment. Gloating even more than usual, Russo sauntered over to Brodsky, who looked ghastly pale. By now, everyone had seen Jennifer O'Neil's decapitated head floating inside a jar.

"Looks like I was right about Anna all along," Russo whispered in Brodsky's ear.

"But how?" a random officer asked.

"Easy. Access panels," Russo answered while shining his flashlight toward the attic's former secret. "Super easy to remove, not to mention the perfect way to frame someone else for murder."

The Chief glanced between Russo's smug expression and Brodsky's grim visage. No matter what the truth turned out to be, he only had one move to make.

"Put out an APB for Anna Collins, previously assumed to be abducted. Tell all units to approach with caution and arrest her on sight," he said into the police radio. Despite following protocol, something about this entire incident didn't feel right. Anna was the least likely murder suspect in his entire career, and he didn't trust Russo or Blake. Would they go to such desperate extremes to protect their reputation?

Two hours later, Brodsky's stomach turned. He'd been back in the police station for less than a minute before one of the forensic lab tech experts called him into her office.

"What's going on?" he asked.

Jane lost herself in his eyes for a beat before recovering her professionalism. *This is going to hurt,* she thought. "I hate to tell you this...but I found some blood on that Anna Collins hoodie. It...well, it's a match for O'Neil's blood, sir."

His face slackened. *This is a nightmare.* "You're sure?"

She confirmed his fears with a sympathetic nod.

"It doesn't make any sense."

"What doesn't make any sense?" Russo asked as he sauntered into the room without knocking.

She wanted to hide the evidence for Brodsky's sake but knew that wasn't an option. Unhappily, she handed the paperwork to Russo. Jane had to let him know, but that didn't mean she had to say it again.

Russo's eyes widened and his typical smug grin returned. *I knew it!* Confidence and bravado rushed back into his body with equal measure as he stared at the indisputable proof of Anna's guilt.

"Sorry to say I told you so, Brodsky, but…no, you know what? I'm not sorry at all," he chuckled. "Boy did you put all your chips on the wrong horse this time."

Russo reached out to pat Brodsky's shoulder in a condescending manner. His hand fell short by a few feet as the detective quickly moved away.

"Don't be such a sore loser, Brodsky."

"This isn't over yet. Not by a longshot. She had blood on her hoodie. So what? That could mean they were both attacked by the same person."

"Whatever you say, man," Russo laughed again.

CHAPTER FORTY-TWO

"In a surprising twist, our sources tell us the police are now looking at Anna Collins as a suspect in the murder of Jennifer O'Neil. We asked for more information, but the Chief of Police refused to comment. Is the woman we once presumed to be a victim actually responsible for all the recent murders? As soon as we learn more, we'll let you know. Be sure to keep your TV tuned to..."

Anna's sister stared at the TV in shock and anger. She'd just tossed her shoe at it, but fortunately, the expensive flat screen hadn't broken. She reached for her phone and called the non-emergency police line.

"I need to talk to Detective Brodsky."

"He's not here right now, ma'am."

"Then maybe you can tell me what the hell is going on? Why is the news saying that my sister Anna is a killer? That's so many kinds of wrong that I don't even know where to start. Are you all stupid or just incompetent?"

The officer on phone duty closed his eyes and counted to five. He hated the way people always seemed to be yelling at him whenever he picked up the phone.

"I assure you, ma'am, that we're..."

"No," Liz cut him off. "I assure *you* that you have no idea what the hell you're talking about." She hit end before tossing her phone at the wall.

"Idiots!" she screamed while mentally chiding Anna for getting herself wrapped up in this entire mess to begin with. *If you'd only listened to me and moved out of that crime-infested hellhole. Dammit, Anna!*

* * * * *

Anna's mouth could no longer conjure up enough saliva to keep her throat from hurting. It had been at least a day since her captor had tossed water at her. Her strength waned as thirst, hunger, and body aches took over her senses.

Rough hands grabbed her mouth and forced it open long enough to slip a gag inside. Anna tried to struggle, but every movement sent thunderbolts of neuropathy and joint pain through her limbs. Hearing returned to her right ear with a discordant pop, and she realized the earplug had been ripped free.

"Stop squirming or this'll get a lot worse," a deep, dangerous voice warned her before roughly shoving the earplug back in place.

Anna didn't want to die, but she also understood her abductor's words contained some wisdom. She couldn't get free anyway, and even if she did, she'd have to deal with being handcuffed, blindfolded, and gagged. *I need to wait for a better opportunity. I hope I get one...*

Her body was dragged across something wooden. The hard edges of the unknown surface kept ramming into her side. She could barely suppress the screams of pain that longed to burst free from her lips. The surface eventually smoothed out, but this didn't provide any comfort. Instead, a scratchy fabric encased her body at an awkward angle before her form rose into the air beneath the strength of four arms.

Nausea took hold before Anna was mercifully placed back on a flat surface a couple of minutes later. She knew she'd been moved to a new location. The big question was why?

A gentle vibration moved through her body. *Uh oh.*

The car Anna couldn't see or hear took off quickly, tossing her around its spacious trunk. Motion sickness instantly made the nausea of a few minutes ago seem like a welcome memory. She hoped the ride would be over before the gag caused her to choke to death on her own vomit.

The rhythmic motion of the car's tires came to a halt approximately ten minutes later. A zipper Anna couldn't hear revealed her skin.

"Do it," a voice hissed in the darkness.

A needle jabbed into a vein on Anna's leg. Her muffled scream couldn't be heard more than a few feet away, but it reverberated through her head like a rifle blast.

Anna's body relaxed, and the two people staring at her smiled.

* * * * *

"911. What's your emergency?"

"There's a woman passed out on my lawn!"

"Do you know her, sir?"

"No. She looks rough, though. She wouldn't wake up, even when I shook her."

"An ambulance is on the way, sir."

* * * * *

24 Hours Later

Anna's eyes fluttered open and recoiled from the harsh light above her hospital bed. She tried to move and found herself cuffed to a bar. Confused, she experimented with her hearing and speech. Both seemed to work fine. *Why am I still handcuffed? And where are my glasses?*

A uni stirred in the corner of the room. "She's waking up," he announced quietly into the police radio on his shoulder.

"Where am I?" Anna asked.

"The hospital," the uni responded.

"What happened?"

"I'm sorry, ma'am, but you'll need to hold your questions for the detective, okay? I'll let the nurse know you're up." He walked out of the room but returned almost instantly.

"How are you feeling, Anna?" a kindly-voiced woman in green scrubs inquired.

"Like I got run over by about twenty semi-trucks," she groaned.

The nurse chuckled. "As bad as all that, huh? Maybe I'd better turn up your morphine drip, then."

"Are you sure that's a good idea?" the uni asked. "She needs to be able to answer some questions."

"No, what she needs is to get some rest so she can heal."

The uni knew he'd never win this argument. He decided to let the detectives handle it.

The door opened under the impatient force of Brodsky's hand. He looked down at Anna; she seemed so small and fragile in comparison to the medical machines flanking her bed. His heart hurt at the sight of her bruises, and the handcuffs overwhelmed him with shame and anger. *How dare that S.O.B. do this to her?*

Russo wouldn't let his cockeyed idea rest. Chief Brower had informed Brodsky that he and Jones would have to go along with it, for now. Brodsky couldn't be positive, but he had an inkling that the Chief had no doubt about Anna's innocence. So, why go through this charade?

"It's good to see you awake," he said. This barely scratched the surface of his thoughts and feelings on the subject. How could Brodsky tell her he'd been unable to sleep since she'd disappeared and he'd blown off his ex-girlfriend for the last time because he couldn't stop thinking about her?

"Why am I handcuffed?"

"That's for your protection." He didn't like lying, but he'd also been warned not to upset her. "More importantly, can you tell me what happened?"

"I don't really know. I remember sitting at the dining room table in the safe house, reading a book. The next thing I knew, I woke up handcuffed and blindfolded."

"Any idea how you ended up passed out on a lawn?"

"They put me in the trunk..."

"They?"

"Yeah, I'm pretty sure it was two people. I'm sorry, I'm really thirsty. Can I get a drink of water?"

"Of course," he said.

"Thank you." She gulped down the entire plastic cup of water before continuing. "Anyway, they drove for a while, I'm not sure how long. I think they drugged me with a needle? That's all I remember."

"A needle? Where did they inject it, do you know?"

"I think...my right leg."

Brodsky asked the nurse to help him examine her for a needle mark.

"There's one," the nurse pointed at Anna's calf.

"Will that be there for a while?"

"Hard to say," the nurse answered.

Brodsky took a photo of it with his smartphone, followed by firing off a text to Jones. "The department's photographer is going to come visit you shortly, okay, Anna? He'll get a better photo of the injection site."

"Okay," she replied hazily.

"You need to go now, Officer," the nurse said.

"Detective," Brodsky answered distractedly.

CHAPTER FORTY-THREE

"I got the background check back on all of Anna's close friends, family members, and everyone else who could potentially be involved in the case" Jones told his partner.

"And?"

"Look at this."

"You're kidding me, right?"

"Nope. It's all there in black and white."

"I can't believe he used to live in Tennessee and we're just now finding out."

"That's not all, boss. If you take a look at this timeline from the past decade, he apparently loves to move from place to place. More than half of them have unsolved serial murders, too."

"Son of a bitch," Brodsky said. He picked up the paperwork and headed into the Chief's office to plan their next move.

"Bring her into custody when she's released from the hospital."

"But, Chief..."

"It's what's best for everyone at the moment. Look on the bright side; she's not going to get abducted again from a holding cell. And this might help us flush him out at the same time."

Word circulated around the station quickly, but only Brodsky, Jones, and Chief Brower knew Anna wasn't a viable suspect. Unsurprisingly, Russo launched into gloat mode.

"I *knew* she wasn't on the up and up. My instincts were screaming it, and they're never wrong."

"Except for the Dellmond mess, you mean," Jones bit back on his partner's behalf.

Russo ignored Jones and kept ribbing Brodsky about having a crush on a serial killer. "Your instincts are clearly shit, man. Seems like it may be time to turn in your badge."

Brodsky's determination to help Anna make it to other side of this fiasco with her reputation intact mattered more to him than taking Russo's bait. He left the room without saying a word, and Russo's face screwed up in anger.

"Your partner's a mental case, Jones."

Jones followed Brodsky's lead, but he still allowed himself to daydream about meeting up with the uncouth agent in a dark alley. *This'll all be over soon,* Jones reminded himself.

* * * * *

"What's our next move?" Jones asked.

Corvo Hollows

Without answering, Brodsky quickly reversed and drove out of the station much faster than the posted speed limit. The police radio crackled to life.

"We've got a hit on the latest APB the Chief called in, Brodsky. The vehicle is currently moving southbound on I-275 near the airport. Should we engage?"

"No, just keep an eye on it and *don't* lose them. Got it?"

"10-4."

Brodsky merged onto 275-S off of Ford Road. Blue and red lights illuminated the outside as he abandoned the vehicle's typical incognito mode in favor of speed. They were fifteen miles behind their quarry, but that didn't mean much when the other driver had no idea someone was in pursuit.

The speedometer broke one-hundred, and Brodsky showed no signs of slowing down. Jones imagined the car lifting off the freeway and flying over the traffic ahead. At this pace, he was almost convinced the vehicle had sprouted wings.

They passed the exit for the airport in half the normal time, which put them within ten miles of their goal. If they didn't make up the difference soon, they'd risk running out of time. The Ohio border sat a mere fourteen miles away. They were already out of their jurisdiction and would need to call in the State Police or the feds as it was. Letting the other car cross into Ohio would take its occupants out of their range altogether.

"Hold on," Brodsky commanded as his foot somehow pressed down even more. Meanwhile, Jones called the State Police near the border to let them know their help was required.

259

Another update confirmed that Brodsky had pulled within three miles of the unsuspecting car, but now a new problem arose. If they kept their police lights on, the driver might get spooked and take off. At the same time, it would also become impossible to warn other motorists of their reckless speed. Deciding to risk it, Brodsky flipped the lights off and continued weaving in and out of traffic at more than one-hundred miles per hour.

The reason for the one-sided chase came into view, and Brodsky allowed himself a slight smile. He was going to get answers, dammit, and he knew in his gut that Anna would be completely exonerated. After everything she'd been through, this was the least he could do for her.

As planned, a couple of state troopers pinned the vehicle in question within a moving road block. Brodsky came up from behind, forcing the car to either stay in position or swerve off the road. All three police vehicles lit up in sync, and the freeway became bathed in red and blue strobes.

For a second, it looked like the driver was contemplating an off-roading excursion, but the car eventually came to a stop on the side of the freeway.

Brodsky approached the driver's side of the vehicle with a State Trooper by his side. Jones and the other officers pulled their guns.

The car's window rolled down, and Brodsky shined his flashlight inside. "Can I help you?" the driver asked.

"I need you to step out of the vehicle, sir."

"Wait, this is crazy," the passenger said.

"Sir? I need you to listen to me right now. Step out of the vehicle."

"Detective Brodsky?" the man asked as he pulled himself free of the driver's seat.

"Yes. Turn around, please." Brodsky pushed the man against the side of the door, followed by patting him down.

"What's this all about?"

Handcuffs were slipped around Jaxon's wrists. "You're under arrest for the abduction of Anna Collins and the murder of…"

Jaxon's mind went blank with panic. Fear drowned out the names being read to him and he desperately looked to his passenger, Rene, for help. "You know I didn't do this!"

Rene's frightened countenance shook Jaxon to the core. She clearly wasn't going to come to his rescue. After Jaxon was roughly placed into the back of Brodsky and Jones' vehicle, they asked a State Police officer to transport Rene to the Canton Police Station for questioning.

Russo and Blake glared as Jaxon was brought into the station and taken directly to an interrogation room.

"What's this all about?" Russo asked.

"If you'd done any actual detective work, you'd know," Brodsky spat at him before slamming the door in Russo's face.

"Why did you do it, Jaxon?"

"I didn't!"

"Bullshit!"

"I love Anna. Why would I hurt her?"

"I'm guessing for the same reason you've hurt people in your last five or six states."

"What are you talking about?"

"The fact that you have DMV records in Tennessee and several other states," Jones piped up. "And each of those states just so happens to have had an active serial killer during your residency."

Jaxon's eyes threatened to bulge out of his head. A bead of sweat moved its way down his back and his hands tremored slightly. "I've never lived anywhere but Michigan."

"That's not what our records say."

"Well, your records are wrong, then. Maybe they were hacked or something, I don't know, but I didn't do *anything!*"

Brodsky didn't want to hear excuses. His anger had reached the tipping point, and Jones could feel an imminent explosion in the air. Yet Jones was also conflicted; what if Jaxon wasn't lying? His words seemed improbable, but they had the strong ring of truth to them.

"Can I see you outside for a second?" Jones asked his partner.

Brodsky grunted but moved toward the door. "This isn't over," the detective barked over his shoulder.

"What is it, Jones?"

His partner's challenging eyes and authoritative stance brought a lump into Jones' throat. Swallowing hard, he said, "I don't think he's lying."

Brodsky's face turned red and he slammed his right fist into his left palm. "You might be right, kid," he answered bitterly. "My gut says it's not him. But who the hell is it, then?"

Taking a beat to cool off, the detectives reported to the front desk to find out where Rene had been taken.

"No State Troopers have been here this evening. Sorry."

"That makes no sense. They should have been here a while ago," Brodsky began. Then comprehension dawned in his eyes. "Oh, my god...Get them on the radio. Quick!"

Neither vehicle answered, but another State Police Officer spoke up. "Sorry, Canton. There's been some type of accident with our boys on I-275 N, just before Ford. We're en route now."

Brodsky and Jones didn't need to speak. They both immediately ran outside. Tires squealed as they peeled out of the lot. Other nearby drivers jammed on their brakes, barely avoiding a series of near-accidents.

The stench of the accident hit their nostrils before they stepped back into the open air. The two State Police cars had combined to form an indecipherable mess of plastic steel, smoke, and flames. Rescue personnel were on the scene, and they'd pulled four officers free of the wreckage.

"Where's the woman?" Brodsky shouted, but none of the officers were in any condition to respond. The detective grabbed one of the EMTs and shouted over the roar of the fire, "What happened to the woman?"

"What woman? We didn't find anyone but these four officers."

"Is it possible she's still trapped inside?"

"Yeah...but if so, she's likely incinerated by now."

CHAPTER FORTY-FOUR

Two Weeks Later

"The final EMT and coroner report have been released in this bizarre case. They prove that the main suspect, Rene Raby, was in the second vehicle, but authorities have been unable to find any of her teeth or bones. Fortunately, one of the officers' body cams survived the inferno, and it captured more than enough for officials to have issued a warrant for her arrest.

"In her chilling accidental testimony, which you can hear exclusively on Channel 7 tonight, Mrs. Raby gloated that she'd "kill all of you." Her last words, "too bad I can't keep your heads...or your hands," are being seen by many as an admission of guilt in the serial murders. Within five seconds of this final statement, the secondary car crashed into the lead one. Tragically, all four State Troopers died in the fiery crash.

This is Diane Douglas, reporting live from Canton."

The click of a remote plunged Anna's living room into darkness. She'd been released, despite Russo's continual complaints, but her last lingering sense of safety was shattered.

What the news hadn't reported yet was the evidence that had been found in Rene's attic. She was almost certainly the killer, and she'd also been Anna's abductor. All that time, Anna had been held only a few feet from her own apartment. Dealing with that information hadn't been easy, nor had the betrayal and disappearance of someone Anna had considered to be a real friend.

Jaxon's story about being framed turned out to be true. He'd given the police everything from his birth certificate to various paystubs to prove he'd always lived in Michigan. An IT security specialist also found evidence that the DMV records had been hacked.

None of this mattered, though; Anna could no longer stand to be in the same room with him. The memories were too painful, especially the treasonous act he'd admitted to.

"I'm really sorry," he'd said with a hangdog expression and tears in his eyes. "I never should have gone along with it. But Rene convinced me you were having some type of mental illness relapse, and I just wanted to help."

"What did you do?" Anna had demanded.

"I told you I didn't hear the noises...but I actually did. One of the two times, anyway. I started thinking maybe I was hearing stuff, too, but that's no excuse for not being honest with you."

Anna and Jaxon parted ways permanently that day. She missed him, but she knew she'd never be able to trust him again. Jeani told her she'd made the healthiest choice for her mental health, and she took comfort from her decision being therapist approved. Of course, her sister also supported her choice, although she hadn't put it quite as nicely as Jeani had.

Her heart seized as knuckles rapped on the front door. Taking a deep breath, she reminded herself that she knew someone was coming over. She stood back and allowed Brodsky to enter the newly opened door. He smiled and carefully removed his shoes.

"Hi, Anna."

"Hi," she replied. Brodsky had feelings for her, and she knew it. He also understood she was nowhere near ready to date again. But it couldn't hurt to be friends, right? Besides, who knew what the future might hold?

EPILOGUE

Rene's hand surfed the wind waves from the passenger side window. They'd gotten away with it once again, and she wanted to celebrate. "It was so nice of Uncle Sam to teach you all about hacking," she tittered while contemplating Jaxon's fate.

"I never thought I'd say this, but I'm actually glad I enlisted," her husband responded. Unlike the story she'd told Anna, James had been discharged from the military five years ago after specializing in military hacking.

"Where to next?" Rene asked.

James grinned at the possibilities. "I've got two new passports for us, plus a bottle of hair dye. But this time, wherever we go, let's stay somewhere together, okay?"

She nodded in agreement as her thoughts darkened. Their marriage had been one of shared psychopathic convenience for years, but she didn't want to actually shack up with James.

She was supposed to fit in like a dutiful but flirtatious military wife, and his role was to stay hidden when they weren't taking care of business. If James wanted to renegotiate the terms now, she might have to steal a move from his playbook by adding his hand to her next trophy collection.

Her only regret during their five years of fun was hurting Anna. She couldn't bring herself to kill the one woman she'd come to think of as a real friend, so she'd framed that idiot Jaxon instead.

Rene had been furious when she'd found out her husband had slapped Anna. Even if she let him live, she'd have to teach him a lesson. He needed to remember who was in charge, now and always.

"Let's go somewhere isolated. I want to have some fun together of a different kind this time," she giggled flirtatiously. "And maybe we'll get lucky and run into some campers we can kill. Just remember; you can kill as many guys as you'd like, but the women are all mine."

Thank you for reading Corvo Hollows! If you enjoyed this book, please post a review to Amazon, Goodreads, and/or Bookbub. Your reviews make a big difference, and they're all greatly appreciated!

Want to find out which parts of this book were based on a real-life story? Be sure to check out the Author's Note.

Looking for a new book to read? My bibliography includes an award-winning, #1 Amazon bestselling Gothic Horror Novel, a humorous Paranormal Mystery Series, and two dark, reimagined Fairy Tales. Learn more by continuing past the Author's Note.

AUTHOR'S NOTE

I hope you enjoyed reading Corvo Hollows as much as I enjoyed writing it! Although the serial killings were fictional, the inspiration for this story came from a very dark place. Almost everything from the first chapter was taken from a real-life incident involving one of my closest friends.

She did have an extremely weird couple stop at her house after a woman yelled for help. That woman also really did try to get into my friend's house, and the screen door did get stuck. Even freakier is the fact that the couple did move into her community a few days later, and they did attempt to change their physical appearance with haircuts, etc. They no longer live there, and as far as we know, they weren't actually stashing any drugs – or body parts – in their house.

Everything else in this book, aside from some of the settings taken from the real-life area, is completely fictional. For example, Canton, MI, has never had a real-life serial killer. In fact, it's a very nice community with an extremely low violent crime rate. At the time of this writing, it's been ten years since a homicide took place within the city limits.

If you enjoyed this book, please share it with your book-loving friends and post a review to Amazon and your favorite book review sites. Reviews are the single best way to thank an author, and they help us continue to write and release more books.

Are you looking for your next read? Please check out the book excerpts after this note. Also, if you're looking for another thriller book, I highly recommend the following authors: Mark Edwards, Peter Swanson, Matthew FitzSimmons, and Sarah Pinborough.

You can reach out to me via social media with any questions or comments:

www.twitter.com/aprilataylor
www.facebook.com/aprilataylorhorror
www.instagram.com/aprilataylorwriter

Sign up for my newsletter to learn about new releases. You'll also occasionally receive special deals and free stories! www.aprilataylor.net

ACKNOWLEDGEMENTS

As always, I want to say thank you to Anne, Kristen, and everyone else who continuously supports my writing. Also, a big thank you to the person who gave me permission to write about her real-life story.

Thanks are also due to Tina and Christina for being a big part of my early readers/beta readers team!

I also feel like I'd be remiss if I didn't acknowledge the real-life couple that inspired this book. I'm glad you no longer live near my friend (whew!), and I hope that you never scare someone like that again.

THE HAUNTING OF CABIN GREEN: A MODERN GOTHIC HORROR NOVEL

Welcome to Cabin Green, where the setting is familiar, but the story is completely unexpected.

Going to Cabin Green alone after the death of his fiancée was Ben's first mistake. His second mistake was tempting fate by saying, "There's no such thing as an evil building." Now he's caught in a nightmare of his own making deep in the woods of Northern Michigan. Even worse, a family history of mental illness makes it impossible for him to know if the ghosts haunting the cabin are real or all in his head.

This modern Gothic horror story takes the reader directly into Ben's hellish experience. Is he crazy? Is a ghost haunting him? The only way to find out is to make it to the end of this deep, dark thrill ride that's filled with more twists than a roller coaster.

More than 3,500 readers have checked in to Cabin Green. Don't miss your reservation for this unique Gothic nightmare.

One of PopSugar's Most Chilling Horror Books of 2018.
One of Inquisitr's Best Horror Books of 2018.
One of Ranker's 2018's Scariest Horror Books.
One of BoredPanda's 7 Books That Scared Me Half to Death.
#1 Amazon Best-Seller in Ghosts, Gothic, U.S. Horror, & LGBT Horror.

MISSING IN MICHIGAN: ALEXA BENTLEY PARANORMAL MYSTERIES BOOK ONE

Is she a medium? A psychic? Alexa Bentley only knows one thing for certain; she can talk to ghosts. And sometimes, they take her advice. *Missing in Michigan* is ideal for fans of the *Sookie Stackhouse Southern Mysteries,* quirky female characters, and the Paranormal Mystery/Supernatural Suspense genre. This exciting, funny series will keep you guessing!

Alexa's unusual ghost therapy skills take her to a remote corner of Michigan's Upper Peninsula. But this case is much trickier than anything else she's ever encountered. A grieving ghost, several missing teens, and a supernatural creature from Native American folklore stand in her path. Along the way, she manages a bit of romance and lots of witty humor.

Followed by:

Book Two – Frightened in France
Book Three – Lost in Louisiana

VASILISA THE TERRIBLE: A BABA YAGA STORY (MIDNIGHT MYTHS & FAIRY TALES BOOK 1)

This clever, dark reimagining of Vasilisa the Beautiful is ideal for fans of The Bear and the Nightingale, Wicked, and Maleficent.

A small village is filled with fear after Vasilisa reports seeing a witch in the nearby cursed woods. Neighbors turn on each other, the land turns bone dry, and bodies begin to pile up. Baba Yaga quickly becomes the primary suspect. Meanwhile, Vasilisa uses her beauty and charisma to bewitch the minds and hearts of every other villager. But is she truly a witch or is something else responsible for all of the mayhem?

Fairy tales depict Vasilisa as beautiful, brave, and fair. But what if terrible was a better description? Baba Yaga has been called everything from a murderous witch to an ambivalent guardian between the living and the dead. But what if she was simply an observant, skeptical elderly woman who was cast out of society for being different? Vasilisa the Terrible: A Baba Yaga Story encourages readers to look beyond the attractive surface to find the ugly evil hidden within.

This dark, reimagined fairy tale was created with adults in mind, although it's also suitable for most young adults. Vasilisa the Terrible is not intended for young children, unless you're comfortable sharing the darker, gruesome fairy tale style with them that was exhibited in the original, uncensored Grimms' Fairy Tales.

Vasilisa the Terrible: A Baba Yaga Story is the first Kindle Short Read in the Midnight Myths and Fairy Tales series. This story is 11,000+ words.

Followed by:

Book Two - Death Song of the Sea: A Celtic Story

Made in the USA
Las Vegas, NV
30 June 2023

74096675R00163